Precious Mate

....

Richard Clups

Copyright © 2024 by Richard Clups

All rights reserved.

No portion of this book may be reproduced in any form without written permission from the publisher or author, except as permitted by U.S. copyright law.

Contents

1. Prologue — 1
2. The Girl — 3
3. Declaration — 6
4. The Fight — 10
5. Their Mark — 15
6. Recovery — 19
7. Afterwards — 24
8. Red Eyes — 30
9. Rescue — 35
10. Run — 39
11. Is This War? — 45
12. His Return — 50
13. Defeat — 57
14. Unmarked — 64
15. Why Did This Happen? — 70

16.	Hospitalized	76
17.	Announcement	81
18.	Forgiveness	85
19.	Respect	91
20.	I'm Home	95
21.	Epilogue	98
22.	Happy Epilogue	104

Prologue

"Hey," I said cautiously, scared to make the first move.

Thankfully, I didn't have to make it. Luca stepped forward and took me by the waist, pulling me close to him. A jealous snarl ripped from Anthony's chest. Did he just growl? What the hell's going on here?!

Luca leaned closer to me, ignoring Anthony. "I'm not good with words like these. But you know that, Mavis." He smiled gently while his eyes filled with an emotion - love?- that caused butterflies in my stomach. A warm feeling surrounded my heart. Did it just speed up?

"So, this is the only way I can describe it."

He suddenly leaned his head down and captured my lips in a long kiss. It was gentle, yet harsh. He claimed my lips as his own, taking complete control. He made a possessive noise into the kiss. making my heart fill with affection.

I was suddenly jerked from him and a second body wrapped around me possessively. It was Anthony.

And he looked pissed.

Mavis, a young teenage human girl, lived a life of normalcy with her five best friends. But when these men reveal their true forms and claim her as their mate, she realizes the world is filled with not just humans, but hidden supernaturals. And her five 'best friends' aren't as innocent as she thought.

The Girl

Mavis

    Sunlight shone through the cafeteria as I plopped down my tray on the table and sat down. I began to pick up my hamburger when I heard a familiar voice.

"Mavis!" It was Mason (my best friend). Well, one of my best friends.

He perched on the bench next to me as we playfully shared a fist bump.

"Whats up Mason?" I jeered while bumping shoulders with him playfully. He bumped back playfully, his smile seemed to radiate pure happiness.

"Nothing much. Physics sucks ass though." He sighed before rubbing his hand over his blond locks, his green eyes suddenly becoming tired.

I patted his shoulder in mock sympathy. I sigh tiredly, "School will be over soon. Just another year." He groaned, resting his forehead against the wooden table. "School is torture," he muttered, before closing his eyes and drifting off.

"Hey Mavis." I turned my head back around behind me. I spotted the boys, Leo, Luca, Anthony, and Dylan. All of my best friends. I smiled brightly, pointing with my thumb down at Mason who was fast asleep. The boys all chuckled to themselves. We all knew how lazy Mason could be.

They sat down at the table as we began to talk about our classes.

I met these boys when I was just three years old, thirteen years ago. We met at the park, and us being innocent children, we all decided to play together. Mason with his green eyes and blond hair, Leo with his black hair and eyes. Luca with his blond hair and blue eyes. Anthony with his brown hair and golden eyes. And Dylan with his brown hair and brown eyes. We were total opposites yet we were all the same. We became best friends instantly and we always had each others' backs. I love them like they're my brothers. At least, I think.

Suddenly, the entire cafeteria began to quiet down and as if on cue the school's bad boy, Jesse Davidson, strode through the cafeteria. I turned my glare towards him which he turned his eyes to immediately. He sent one of his 'killer smiles' which seemed to "make every girl in the room faint". Such bullshit.

He stalked towards our table, a spark of interest gathering in his sharp eyes. He seemed to give the boys a passing glance, even though they were glaring daggers at him. I tried my best to hold back a laugh but I was failing.

He stopped in front of me and leaned down to face me. He smirked and leaned a bit closer, making me shut up immediately, and send him a death glare. He just smirked more, which pissed me off greatly. "Hey there, Mavis," he said smoothly, kissing me on the cheek unexpectedly. It caught me off guard and I started, barely understanding what happened before I saw Leo and Luca jump up, hostility burning off of them. Leo stared daggers at Jesse and grabbed the back of Jesse's jacket, making Jesse turn and face him. His smirk immediately left his face, a look of hate rested on Jesse's golden eyes.

Luca stood in front of me and shoved Jesse back further. Jesse then looked at Luca, who wasn't backing down for anything. I watched my two friends handle Jesse, shock still resting on my face.

I was about to stand up, when a flashing pain went off in the back of my head. It was a soccer ball?! Why can't the jocks stop throwing those around. It seriously hurts people. I groaned, my temples throbbing. I could barely keep my eyes open, to see Leo's worried face, before collapsing and completely blacking out.

_

"I have to tell her. I can't hold back my feelings for her. I love her too much."

I squinted my eyes, before reality hit me, and I remembered everything. Wait, what did I just hear?

"I know how you feel. I love Mavis, too. But we can't just spring it on her." That was definitely Anthony. And did he just say he loved me??

"I agree. But I want to tell her badly. I know she loves us too," Luca murmured and Leo agreed. I kept my eyes closed, pretending to be asleep. I needed to hear this.

"I want to be with her," Mason murmured.

"I want to be with her too," Dylan whispered. I could see the boys agreeing.

I could feel the sleepiness pulling me back in. It was almost too hard to resist, and right as I accepted the darkness, Mason's voice broke through my hazed spell.

"Then let's claim her."

Declaration

Mavis

Nerves hit me like steel. I woke up in my bed, every muscle in my body tensed. I remember everything. That was not a dream. Which means only one thing.

My best friends are going to declare their love for me.

A new feeling ripples throughout my body. I'm not even sure how I feel about them romantically!

Fear gripped my heart. I didn't want to hurt them. Maybe I could pretend to be sick? No, that wouldn't work. I'm good at acting, but I'll have to face them sooner or later.

I wish it was later though.

_

I made my way through the front doors of the school, wearing my faded skinny jeans, thick black sweater, and a pair of white converse.

I looked around, making sure I was alone before sighing in relief.

I shouldn't have gotten my hopes up.

I suddenly felt a light tap on my shoulder. I squeaked in surprise, jerking around to see Luca and Anthony there. I smiled cautiously, fear filling my heart along with another emotion I didn't understand.

"Hey Mavis!" Luca yips in excitement as he nudged Anthony gently. Anthony's eyes widened for a split second, nervousness basically spilling from his pores. He gave a small smile, clearing his throat nervously.

"At the end of school, could you meet us on the roof to talk about something?" He nervously stuttered out. It was obvious he was a bit scared of what I would say.

I knew what was going to happen. I was terrified. But thank goodness I'm a great actress.

"Sure." I smiled, masking my true feelings. They wanted to meet with me? Oh no.

Anrhony smiled gently, cupping my face with one hand and staring into my eyes. My heart began to beat faster.

What is he doing?

Why am I so nervous?

What is this feeling?

Notincing my anxiousness, Anrhony smiled evilly, before releasing me slowly to turn to walk away.

When he disappeared behind a corner, I realized Luca was still standing there.

I turned to him quickly to see him watching me, anger brimming in his eyes. He grabbed my hand aggressively and pulled me into a hug. He rested his head in the crook of my neck, making me blush. My heart wouldn't - couldn't - calm down. I was a giant ball of nerves.

He released me with a cheeky grin, kissing the side of my head gently, making me blush harder.

"I-I'll see you later Luca," I called before turning and sprinting away from him.

"Mavis!" I heard him call behind me, but I kept running, too scared to stop and face him now.

I stopped in front of my English class and made my way inside, thankful that I didn't share any classes with the guys.

_

It was the end of the day. I made my way to the roof, my hands shaking. They were going to confess! How do I reject them? Should I reject them?

I shook my head.

That could wait.

I opened the door to see only Anthony and Luca standing there. Confused, I closed the door, alerting the two that I was there.

They turned around, lust evident in their eyes. My heart did a weird flip and I could swear it started to speed up again.

"Hey," I said cautiously, scared to make the first move.

Thankfully, I didn't have to make it. Luca stepped forward and took me by the waist, pulling me close to him. A jealous snarl ripped from Anthony's chest. Did he just growl? What the hell's going on here?!

Luca leaned closer to me, ignoring Anthony. "I'm not good with words like these. But you know that, Mavis." He smiled gently while his eyes filled with an emotion - love?- that caused butterflies in my stomach. A warm feeling surrounded my heart. Did it just speed up?

"So, this is the only way I can describe it."

He suddenly leaned his head down and captured my lips in a long kiss. It was gentle, yet harsh. He claimed my lips as his own, taking complete control. He made a possessive noise into the kiss. making my heart fill with affection.

I was suddenly jerked from him and a second body wrapped around me possessively. It was Anthony.

And he looked pissed.

"You can't just take her first kiss like that! It should've been me!" He snapped, his anger directing to Luca. Luca only grinned and sent Anthony a deadly look. "She was my love first. That only means I get her first kiss," Luca said. Anthony simply huffed, still upset.

He suddenly pulled me closer and bent down to slam his lips against mine.

It was anything but gentle. Rough, commanding, and full of lust. His kiss took so much control, I could barely breathe. My body was on fire. I could barely keep up.

It seemed to only last a few seconds before another pair of arms pulled me away.

It was Mason, Leo, and Dylan.

And they weren't just pissed.

They were beyond that.

The Fight

Mavis

"What the hell is going on here?!" Leo shouted, rage brimming in his black eyes.

"Why don't you just stay out of it?" Luca replied calmly, but you could see his figure tense up.

"Why were you kissing Mavis?" Dylan shouted. And he never shouted.

"Isnt it obvious? We were confessing to her. And if you want to keep your head, then I suggest you stay out of it," Anthony snarled furiously at the men.

Right as Anthony finished his sentence, Mason jumped forward and punched him square in the jaw. Before I could react, I felt a pair of strong arms wrap around my waist. That's when I finally realized the situation I was in. I screamed and tried to get to the now tussling boys, but Dylan kept his tight hold on me. I screamed and kicked, but his arms were like steel cables. He pulled me closer, making me freeze. He put his nose to my neck and took a deep breath. Was he sniffing me?!

He let out a deep sigh and hugged me tighter, pressing his large frame into my small figure. I could've sworn I heard him say, "You smell just like roses."

The boys seemed to stop and were all watching Dylan with mixed looks of jealousy and anger. Leo turned back to Luca and Anthony. "She wasn't yours first. She was mine," he spat out. I screamed in frustration and the boys quit their scuffling, looking back at me.

"Would you stop it?! I'm not some object you can claim because you feel like it!" I snapped, glaring at each boy. I shoved Dylan away from my shaking body. "You can't just declare your love for me and expect me to share those feelings! Especially if you all decide to declare your 'affections' at the same time! Don't even try that shit with me!" I shouted, turning around to scramble away from them.

I shoved open the metal roof door and jumped down the flights of stairs easily. I have to thank my hurdling skills for that.

I pounded down the rest of the stairs, moving to the front of the school. I slowed to a walk and pushed through the front doors to feel the chilly air of the fall weather. It never really bothered me though.

Just as I started my walk home, I heard a voice shout out my name.

"Mavis! Hold on!"

I didn't bother to turn around or stop. Because I knew whose gravelly voice that was.

It was Leo's.

I heard the sound of footsteps. But these footsteps sounded odd, like nails clicking against the concrete. In confusion, I swiveled my head around.

I shouldn't have.

A giant dog, no, it was a wolf, was on top of Leo, pinning him down. I froze. The wolf had a beautiful light brown coat with molten gold eyes. It was the most beautiful wolf I had ever seen. Leo growled fiercely. But before I could react, he started to reshape. Bones cracking, reshaping, changing. Suddenly, he was a large black-furred, black-eyed wolf. He was at least the size a small pony, but so was the other wolf.

I let out a scream of pure fear, higher than I thought my voice could ever go.

The two wolves seemed to ignore me as Leo pushed up against the brown wolf, succeeding in knocking the other male over. The brown wolf twisted on his side and managed to land on his feet. The two giant wolves stood on their two back paws, their two front paws clashing together in an attempt to knock the other away.

I heard a shout from where the brown wolf came from. And, out of nowhere, Mason jumped from the bushes, running towards the two battling wolves.

I was frozen in time, completely unable to move. As soon as Mason spotted me, he froze mid-step and almost fell. He looked like he was about to say something, but he quickly shook his head, turned around, and sprinted once again to the wolves.

He grabbed each wolf by their neck fur and threw the wolves away from each other. I gaped at his intense strength. Since when was he so strong?

"Stop it! Look at where you are!" Mason shouted and both wolves turned their beautiful eyes to me. Fear faded in my mind, leaving curiosity. The wolves shared a guilty look, before lowering their eyes and bounding back to the bushes.

I was always in love with wolves. They were my favorite animal. They were even my second favorite supernatural creature. Werewolves always seemed so cool to me. I never once thought they would be real. I had to be honest, this wasn't scary.

It was amazing.

But that didn't mean I wasn't freaked out by this. I mean, who would've thought they existed? My palms were sweaty and I could feel my heart beating quicker. Even though I knew these guys my whole life, the wolves that stood in front of me terrified me. But I wasn't gonna show them that.

Mason walked slowly to me while giving me a sad look. "Are you okay Mavis?" he asked gently, pulling me into his arms. I nodded, giving him a small smile. "That wasn't fake, was it?"

"No, it wasn't."

"Wow."

He smiled.

"We all knew you loved wolves. We were going to tell you as a group once we told you about our feelings."

I gave him a confused look. "What do you mean? Don't wolves have mates or something? Other wolves that you cherish and love? The only ones in the world you care about? Or were all of those internet pages about werewolves I read wrong?" I asked. He quickly nodded before a blush rose on his face.

"Mavis...you are our mate."

I gave him a startled look. "How? I'm only a human."

He gave me a confused look, before smiling. "I don't know, I just know my wolf is screaming at me to have you, claim you, and keep you away from everyone. Even the guys. And I'm starting to think I shouldn't fight him on it." I blushed madly, keeping my eyes pinned to my feet shyly. "Why?" I managed to squeak out. I was really starting to freak out a bit.

Mason pulled me to his chest and took a deep breath with his nose buried in my neck. He let out a possessive growl, making a small shy smile rise to my lips.

And he said something that made my heart skip a beat.

"Because you're all fucking mine."

Their Mark

Mavis

What did he mean? I was his? Whatever that meant, it had my heart beating twice as fast.

Mason chuckled and drew a hand through his soft blond hair, his green eyes twinkling.

He leaned closer, starting to kiss my neck softly. I bit my lip to hold back a moan of pure pleasure. What was he doing? My friend for so many years... Yet, I didn't want him to stop.

I felt fangs against my neck and closed my eyes, silently trusting him.

He bit down, his fangs digging painfully deep into my neck. I whimpered in pain as Mason pulled away and licked away the blood on his lips. He looked at me, his eyes shining with hunger and possession. He grabbed my hand and took me with him, towards the others.

The bite wouldn't stop hurting. It was throbbing and burning, like my skin was on fire.

It hurt like hell.

Damn these hot boys.

Mason stopped me in front of the guys and they all snapped their heads towards me. We were beside the school now and they all were back in human forms. However, Leo was completely shirtless, showing off his 8-pack. I was fighting to look away, making him smirk. But the smirk quickly faded when he lifted his nose to the air.

He searched my neck and froze when he saw the mark. I covered it in embarrassment, scared of what Leo would do.

He snarled at Mason, his fangs flashing dangerously. "Didn't we talk about how we would all mark her? How could you force that on her?!" He shoved Mason, causing me to huff impatiently.

"Oh, will you stop it? It's already have been an eventful day! Let's just call it a day. And, by the way, I let Mason mark me, because I wanted him to." I scoffed, before turning my back to the boys and marching off, tossing up a hand to wave at the boys. I disappeared behind the school corner and made my way back home, thankful to have to some time to myself.

_

It was Saturday. I woke up from a dreamless sleep and quickly pulled my long brown hair into a messy bun, and glanced down at my light grey tank and plain black sweats. I sighed and rubbed my hand against my neck subconsciously, only to pull away with a hiss at the contact of the bite. Sharp pain radiated throughout my neck. I'm starting to regret this now. How am I supposed to cover this up anyways?

This sucks.

I changed into a pair of dark skinny jeans, and a black blouse before making my way to the hangout I go to meet the guys at every weekend. I hope today isn't an acception to not be there.

To be honest, I was kind of hoping I could ask them about having more than one mate. Because, honestly, I want to be with them all. At least I think...

-

I sat down at our favorite booth, ordering a water. Soon after, Mason, Anthony, Luca, Leo, and Dylan sat down into the booths. Dylan, Mason, and Luca sitting on the other booth. Anthony and Leo sitting next to me.

We all eyed each other as if expecting someone to say something, anything. I finally sighed in defeat, looking at each boy individually.

"I have a question, okay?" I asked cautiously, not able to see if they were up to answering anything. But luckily Luca nodded, ready to answer anything for me. I smiled gently before continuing.

"Is it possible to be marked by more than one wolf? And....mate more than one?" Leo spat out his drink as Dylan started to cough. Mason smirked while Anthony started to laugh. Luca smiled. "It's possible, but unheard of."

I nodded, a slow smile forming on my face.

Once the guys payed the check, we all walked out of the restaurant, wondering around aimlessly.

"Alright. How about we go for a walk?"

We all stood up from the booth and made our way outside, into the snowy wilderness. We made our way to the park while chatting about school and events at home.

Suddenly, Dylan whipped his head to the side, almost abnormally fast. "Everything okay?" Leo asked, unease clinging to him. Dylan nodded slowly, his eyes still focused on a bush from across the park.

I let out a small laugh before I felt a sharp pain invading my stomach. I stopped, scared to look down as a warm liquid trickled down my stomach.

"Mavis?"

"What the hell happened?"

"Fuck!"

"Somebody get a doctor!"

"Dylan, scope the area!"

I was put on the ground, the small stinging pain in my stomach exploding inside of me, sending waves of molten lava through my veins. I looked down slowly to see a knife sticking out of my stomach. Someone just stabbed me.

I felt sick.

Another scream claimed my throat.

Thankfully, no human was in sight.

But the only thing I could think about was Leo's fading figure, begging me to stay with him. But I couldn't. It was too much.

Finally, I closed my eyes, letting the darkness take over my mind.

Recovery

Mavis

The first thing I heard when I came to my senses was a beeping sound. It was constant, healthy. Then the smells came.

It smelled like medication, and I knew that I was in the hospital instantly. I opened my eyes, and took in the area before me. I was in a hospital room, lying on a comfy hospital table, and I had multiple needles in my arms.

I hate needles.

So much.

I slowly pulled the needles out, hissing at the pain, but ignoring the small droplets of blood that followed. I sat up slowly, allowing the dizziness to overpower me.

The dizziness soon faded, and I glanced around the room.

The small doctors room had a small counter in the corner, with a door beside it, which I had assumed was a bathroom.

The rest of the room was plain, with a few chairs beside me, and a tv was mounted to the wall in front of my bed.

I glanced down, feeling thick bandages covering my stomach. I put my hand gently on the bandages that surrounded my stomach and back. It burned, and I hissed once again.

Figures.

And that's when everything came back. The knife, the boys surrounding me, me blacking out.

Someone had tried to kill me.

I nearly blacked out again.

I first racked my brain on who it could've been. It had to have been someone who either hates me, hates the boys, or hates werewolves.

And that's when it clicked.

Hunters. Of course, why didn't I think of it?

And if it isn't Hunters, then someone has some problems.

I flicked the tv to Last Man Standing, and watched the rest of the episode, chuckling at Mandy and Mike. My favorite character was Eve, though.

_

A few hours later, the door opened, and the boys walked in, each one wearing a grim expression.

Dylan had deep circles under his eyes. Mason was pale. Anthony had a stricken expression. Leo seemed to be in pain. And Luca looked as if he saw someone kick a puppy.

"Are you guys okay?" I asked uncertainly. Their eyes snapped to mine, and relief flashed through each of theirs. Dylan ran up - yes, ran up - and kissed me deeply.

I kissed him back gently, and as he pulled away, Anthony shoved him aside. He leaned down, and captured my lips with his. He gained control, and he wrapped his arms around me protectively, before pulling away gently. I smiled, my heart rate picking up.

Leo and Mason seemed to be shoving each other over who would get to kiss me next. Luca took advantage of their bickering, and leaned down next to me, and put his lips on mine. A possessive growl came from the back of his throat when I kissed back. He kissed along my jaw, before taking a shuddering breath, and muttering something like ,"I can't hold back anymore." He grabbed my wrist, and, while putting it to his mouth, brushed his sharp canines against my wrist. I held back a scream of shock, and tried to jerked my wrist away, but his grip stayed.

He dug his teeth into my wrist and silent tears fell down my face.

Before Luca could pull away, he was ripped away from me, causing me to let out a deep, shaky breath.

I turned my head to see Leo trying to punch Luca. Both boys looking pissed.

"STOP IT!"

The two boys stopped, and reluctantly pulled away from each other. I glared at Luca.

"Just let me go home."

_

After going back to my apartment from the hospital, I rested on my soft violet comforter, and watched my friends mates standing around the small area.

They seemed to be murmuring to each other, their gazes dark.

I had decided something in that hospital, too.

While I was out, I mean.

"Leo, Anthony, Dylan," I called out softly.

The boys stopped, and Leo, Anthony, and Dylan came to me.

I let out a small breath of fear, and gave them a look.

They seemed to understand what I was saying, and they circled me.

Anthony started. He bent down, and kissed my collarbone gently, grazing his fangs against my soft skin. I braced myself for the impact, ready to be marked by him.

Anthony

Love filled inside me, and my wolf howled for me to mark her, make her mine. But I knew I had to share her. It's okay, as long as I got her attention.

I burried my fangs inside of her collarbone, tasting her delicious blood in my mouth. I felt her stiffen, and my heart cracked. This must be painful for her. I slowly pulled my teeth out, and licked away her dripping blood.

The urge to keep her for myself started to overpower me. I had to force my wolf back, only to keep my mate safe and happy.

I moved away from her, and watched as Leo and Dylan marked her too. Dylan on her left side of the neck, and Leo on her shoulder. She arched her back slightly, and closed her eyes. When the boys all moved away, we each admired our own mark that rested on her.

I knew these guys would help me protect her. Even if it meant I had to hold myself back, I would keep this beautiful girl, my mate, happy.

Because I love her.

And she's mine.

Afterwards

(Contains Crude Language-More than usual)

-1 month later-

Mavis

After being marked by my mates, I suppose the guys decided for me that I was going to be turned. But I totally agreed with them. Even though I was pissed that they talked about it without me. It was really the only way I could live as long as they could.

The guys had to bring in another werewolf to turn me because apparently mates can't turn one another.

Let me just say, the pain was excruciating. It took 8 hours before I fully turned into a beautiful silver wolf. I was amazed at all of the new scents, sounds, and sights that I had when I turned. As well as the speed, strength, and mind-link. I'm now best friends with my inner-wolf, Uri. I love her so much. She's a diva just like me.

It was all for the best, I couldn't imagine ever being happier.

Luca

I rested in the bed next to my mate. My gentle, kind hearted mate. She is so beautiful.

Ever since the day I marked her with my best friends, we've been nothing short of over-protective.

I think she's still pissed at Leo for punching that one guy at school for looking at her too long.

If Leo hadn't done it, I would've.

Shes mine - ours - and nobody will even think about getting near her now.

We may have marked her, but we never mated with her. She doesn't want us to.

Not yet, at least.

Anthony

Mavis made her way downstairs, moving through the house, our house.

She moved in recently to the house the guys and I had.

And thank goodness she did, otherwise I would've stayed in the apartment with her.

We've been sharing her ever since we marked her, and I regret nothing.

Im so happy that she was my mate. But I was kind of upset that my friends had her too. I wanted her.

But for her, im willing to share.

Leo

As Mavis and the guys ate breakfast, I couldn't help but stare at Mavis... She was stunning.

Luca had her last night, and Dylan had her the night before. It was Anthony's turn tonight.

I miss her.

I haven't had her to myself in a while, and I've been itching to be with her. Even the guys and I set up rules about rotations of who has her when she wasn't home.

But it's rare if she's out alone.

We usually go with her everywhere, just in case.

Because we can't lose her.

I can't lose her.

Dylan

I fought the urge to beat the shit out of Mason, and take Mavis from him.

He pulled her into his arms, and started to kiss her, his hands roaming her body.

I could tell the other guys were pissed off, too.

I stood up, tired of watching Mason with my mate. She's mine, not his.

Why the hell does he think he can just have her?

I pulled Mavis away from Mason, staring into her shocked violet eyes.

They were so beautiful.

I love them.

I love her.

Mason

Why the hell did Dylan pull her away from me?

I pulled my hand through my messy blond hair, my green eyes brimming with rage.

I usually never showed my feelings about Mavis to anyone. But now that she's marked by me, I can't help it.

I want her for myself.

But I guess all of the guys do, too.

Its Saturday, and we had nothing to do.

Mavis wanted to go to the mall, but the guys and I preferred to watch a movie instead.

I smirked when I saw Mavis's scowl.

It was cute.

But I can't help but have this bad feeling inside of me that something is about to happen. Something bad. The guys knew to follow my gut instinct. It never let me down.

So why the hell am I feeling like this?

Mavis

The guys finally agreed to let me walk around the mall alone after hours- or at least it felt like hours- of convincing. Mason seemed a little upset, and I worried for him.

I wonder if everything's okay with him.

Mason pulled into the mall parking lot, and turned to me. He gave me a sad smile, and put his hand over mine.

"Are you sure you want to go shopping?" He asked tiredly, his eyes seeming to darken. I knew it was just because he didn't want anyone near me.

I had to admit, it was hot.

"Yes, I'll be fine," I reassured him, my smile staying on my face. He seemed to relax at my smile, and he smiled back gently, love flashing in his eyes.

I kissed him good-bye, and stepped out of the car. He pulled away, leaving me at the entrance. I walked in, preparing to fight myself against all the sales.

_

I made my way out of Goody's, this being my twelfth store I've come out of. I've been here for at least theee hours, and the guys have been calling me non-stop.

But I answered all of them.

They seemed relieved to hear my voice, and we quickly hung up, before I moved to another store.

As I made my way to the bathroom, I couldn't help but have a small shiver - almost as if someone was watching me. I glanced around, but saw nobody. But I wasn't stupid.

I trust my instincts.

I moved quickly to the bathroom, careful not to draw any attention to me.

Just as I closed to door to the single bathroom, and locked it, a hand came over my mouth. My eyes widened, and fear took over.

A man, who was wearing a hood and mask, appeared next to me. His voice was deep and gravelly as he spoke, "Hello, dear love." I tried to scream, but his hand prevented me from doing so.

I watched him, fear making my eyes tear up. He smiled maliciously, and kissed my neck gently, next to Leo's mark. I shivered in disguist.

"Don't worry. Soon, you'll be with me, love."

Then everything went dark.

Leo

We couldn't find her. She wasn't answering her phone.

Mason knew something was wrong, but he didn't say anything.

What an idiot.

We made our way to the mall, and tracked her scent to the bathrooms. Her scent soon mingled with another scent, a horrid one. We all knew instantly what it was.

Vampire.

A vampire took my mate. Anger coursed through me, but I couldn't do anything, not near these humans.

But I needed my mate.

I needed Mavis.

Where the hell is she?

Red Eyes

Mavis

I woke up, my head throbbing.

There was something soft under me. A bed.

And I felt arms wrapped around me. It was Mason.

It had to be.

My eyes still closed, I turned, and snuggled closer to the warm body, my face coming in contact with his bare chest. A low rumble came from the chest, surprising me. I glanced up, to see red eyes staring back at me, humor and lust burning in them.

I screamed, fear coursing through my body. The man just chuckled, and pulled my body tighter to him. My chest touched his, and I felt his muscles under his shirt flex. We fit together like a glove. It was surprising.

Red Eyes smirked at my expression, before wrapping one hand around my waist and the other around the back of my head.

I watched him fearfully, scared of what he wanted.

When he didn't make any more moves, I decided to look around to find any escape points.

I pushed myself off, and sat up. I glanced around the large room, which was mainly covered in black. Black carpet, black walls, black roof. A tv hung in the middle of the far wall, with couches circling it, and a fire underneath. Furniture circled the room, with three doors sticking out. I'm assuming one was a bathroom, one was a closet, and the other led outside.

Red Eyes pulled me back to him, and let out a moan as my body once again pressed against his.

I scrunched my nose in disguist, and struggled to push away. Once I got to the far side of the bed, he sat up, still smirking, and watched me intently.

The man had black loose hair that hung down his handsome face. He had a sharp jaw that contained a beard, and he had sharp features. His eyes no longer shone red. Instead, they were a beautiful cyan. Inhuman.

"What the hell is this?!" I gestured to the room around me. He let out a laugh, which further fueled my anger. Not innocence, curiosity, or fear. I was pissed.

His smirk grew as he watched me, before replying. "You're in my home, specifically, my room. My name is Alessandro." I huffed, and he raised an eyebrow. "Don't you want to ask the cliche questions? 'Where am I? Who are you? What do you want from me?'" I glared at him once again, before sighing. "Fine. What's with the kidnapping?"

He smiled, and pulled me closer, but not to where we were touching. I felt power pouring from him, which forced my instincts to take over. I started to shake in fear, and he chuckled, before moving a piece of my brown hair behind my ears, and whispering into my ear, "You are so beautiful. And you are mine now."

Luca

Its been three weeks. And no sign of our beautiful girl. We haven't slept a wink, not caring about our own health. We've barely eaten, too worried for our girl. I cuss myself out each and every night for being as stupid as to let her go alone.

Once we get her back, I'll make sure to keep her as mine. She'll never leave my sight.

I sighed, and gripped my hair in stress. A tense Leo sat next to me on the couch in our living room, before he turned his eyes to me. Leo's once powerful and protective black eyes are now dull, and unseeing. I can't help but feel more rage. What the hell was Leo doing? He makes it seem like he's the only one suffering.

I want to kill him.

But I can't do that, it would only hurt my girl. I need her back here. Not only me, but everyone is starting to go insane, craving every piece of clothing and every object she has touched, just for her scent. But now her scent is gone. I'm going insane. I need her here to calm me down.

I need her so badly. But I know I won't get her back until I find her scent trail.

Screw that damned vampire.

Mavis

I placed a plate with steak and mashed potatoes on the side with a small salad in front of Alessandro, and he smiled gently. He pulled me next to him, and claimed my lips roughly, before letting me go. But I didn't kiss back. I gave him a fake smile back, before turning and walking away, my face now filled with disguist.

Three weeks of torture. That's how long I've been here. And every single day, Alessandro has been getting more and more touchy. I can't help but worry about what might happen if he went too far.

I've tried escaping, but that only left him groping me more than necessary, and me crying myself to sleep. I've learned to stay silent and observant. This man is much more terrifying than I thought.

He is a vampire.

Ive become his blood slave.

Apparently the only reason I'm here is because he's needed a blood slave and he chose me. What an idiot.

I know my mates are coming.

And they'll save me. I hope.

Alessandro

Its fake. All of it.

Yes, I want her to be my blood slave, and she is.

But the main reason I have her is because of her mates.

My enemies.

But I've started to do what I told myself I wouldn't. I'm falling in love with her.

Oh shit.

Ive been pushing myself on her, and I know she's terrified. But I can't help it. She's just so beautiful. And her blood is sweeter than I've ever tasted in any other human. Screw that, in any other creature. It satisfies me more than any bagged blood. Now the bagged blood tastes like pure shit. All I can taste is her blood.

Shes just so innocent and funny. But lately she's been quiet. I can tell she's making up another plan. But I can't let her do that. She's mine now. Nobody can take her from me anymore. She's mine only. If those boys even try to take her from me, I will kill them without a second glance. It may have started as a revenge plan, but now I want her. She's my blood slave. And I don't care that those boys are her "mate". They can just find another girl to keep them busy. I don't give a damn.

She wants me. By the end of this, when her mates find her, I'll make her believe it. Whether she wants to or not.

Shes my blood slave now. So I don't care what she thinks. I'm in love with her, and I'm not ready to let go.

Not yet.

Rescue

WARNING: This chapter contains crude and sexual language, and violence. You have been warned.

Mavis

The door opened silently, not alerting me of the presence that rested behind my bed. At the sound of a throat clearing, I whipped my head around. I stared at no other than Alessandro. He smiled lustfully at me.

"You look incredibly sexy in that outfit, little blood slave," he whispered huskily, before gliding towards me. He always seems to be gliding instead of walking like any other normal creature.

I glanced down at my clothes in disguise. You couldn't even call them clothes. I was wearing a tight red silk dress that hugged my body like a second skin, and went down to halfway down my thighs. The top barely went over my sadly large breasts.

I felt violated.

Alessandro rested his hands on my waist, which seemed to crawl lower and rest on my bottom. He chuckled as I flushed, and tried to get out of his grip.

He had been taking about doing the deed, but he had never done it until tonight. I know he's going to do it because this is the most revealing thing I've worn since being here. I literally had nothing on under this dress. Nothing.

He pulled my boy flush against his, and wrapped his arms around me possessively. Fear crawled up my spine. I don't want this. Not now. Not by him.

But my boys will be here soon. I know it.

Once Alessandro started to pull down my dress, I snapped. A loud slap echoes through the room. Alessandro had frozen, his cheek now a bright red in the shape of a handprint. His features turned strict, and he grabbed my wrists roughly.

He started to drag me from the room. Tears streamed down my face. I was terrified of what he was going to do. He dragged me through a doorway, and made his way down a flight of stairs.

He took me to the dungeon. He opened one of the free cages, and ripped my dress off of me. I screamed. The men in other cages who had enough strength left whistled and let out cat-calls. I was flaming and shaking. Alessandro dragged me through the cell, and shoved me against the wall. He slammed his lips against mine. I heard the clink of metal, before I felt the cuffs wrap around my arms and legs. Silver cuffs.

I screamed into Alessandro's mouth. But he just smirked, and backed away. He grabbed a whip off of the table I just now saw, and turned back to me. His eyes gleamed with a hunger that was unknown to me. He lightly traced the whip across my bare body, and I shivered, feeling the leather across my skin. This was going to hurt like a bitch.

Then he pulled back the whip.

Mason

We crashed through the front door. Vampire stench came from all around us. But we already took out everyone.

While we were searching, Anthony and Dylan came upon the scent trail of vampires. We quickly set up, without a plan, and set out immediately. We wanted our girl back ASAP.

We stormed through what looked like a dungeon, and made our way after the scent of our mate. But we all stopped when we smelt it.

Blood.

Mavis

Alessandro set the whip back in it's place. But this time it was covered in blood. My blood.

The tears wouldn't stop flowing down my fave. My entire body was covered in whip cuts. Blood dropped down my limbs, everywhere. All I saw was pain. I didn't realize you could see it, but now I understand you can. Pain was everywhere. I wanted to scream, but that would only cause more pain.

Alessandro moves back to me, and gently cupped my face, the only thing he went easier on. But he still hit it a lot.

He rubbed his thumbs over my cuts, causing me to wince. He shuddered in pleasure. He grabbed my neck, and forced my lips on his. The movement caused me to hiss in pain, but I was blocked from making the noise.

Suddenly, he was shoved off. Relief flooded through me. Standing there was three large wolves. A brown wolf, another brown wolf, and a blonde wolf. They started to tear into Alessandro's screaming body, as two familiar figures rushed to me. Leo and Luca. They quickly unchained me, and wrapped me in their embrace, burying their heads into my neck, and inhaling my scent. They seemed to release their tense breaths, and both hugged me tighter.

Dylan, Mason, and Anthony all came over to me, and each took their turns passing me around and sniffing me. They all seemed to calm down once they confirmed I was actually here. They quickly rushed me or if the house, telling me how much they loved me and soothing things. The cuts and burns stung, which only made me want to knock out.

But with the soothing movement of my boys, it wasn't long until I let the darkness take over.

Run

Mavis

It's been three weeks since I was turned. My wolf, Uri, has been talking nonstop to me. Honestly, I love her.

She's so awesome. She gets me so well, too. And, apparently, she's from a 'beta blood line'. I honestly have no idea what that means, but when I asked Mason, he merely shrugged. "Beta is like the second in line to the alpha in a pack. He controls the pack when the alpha isn't there," he added. I nodded. So the beta is second in charge. That's pretty good. I think?

I made my way downstairs from my room, to get some lunch.

"LUCA!" I screeched, causing a loud banging to go down the stairs, and Luca bursted from the doorway. "WHATS WRONG?" He howled, his eyes scanning the room frantically. I chuckled to Uri mentally, and gave Luca a serious look.

"I want Chick~fil~a."

"What?"

He looked at me in disbelief. I smiled sheepishly. "You heard me." He suddenly smiled, and nodded his head. "I want some too." I sighed. I'm always in the mood for Chick~fil~a.

We made our way to a Chick~fil~a. I got my chicken sandwich, with large waffle fries and dr. Pepper. So yum. I wolfed down the fries hungrily on the way back, and Luca watched me in amusement. When I finished my fries, and took a gulp of my drink, Luca grabbed the sides of my face gently, and jerked me towards him. I was completely caught off guard, as Luca's lips connected with mine. Fire spread through my veins, and Uri became eager and excited. Luca kissed me posessively, and I started to kiss back soon after.

When we broke apart, Luca's eyes were pitch black. He was struggling to keep himself together. I smiled teasingly, and kissed along his jawline. He let out a groan, and his arms circled around my waist possessively.

He crashed his lips to mine. His left arm left my waist, and reconnected on my neck. He began to kiss along the mark he made on my neck, and I held back a moan. He pulled my body closer to his, and growled protectively. His wolf had taken control.

He kissed me softer this time, and gently let me go. I was breathless when he did. I panted heavily, matching his own breaths. His eyes soon turned back to their normal beautiful blue.

There was a dark growl from behind me. We were parked in front of the house, and Anthony and Leo stood behind my side door. I opened the door slowly.

"Whats wrong with you two?" I asked cautiously. Both of their eyes were almost completely black, and they were looking at me.

I walked towards them slowly, and touched both of their arms gently. Their eyes soon turned back to normal, which wasn't much of a difference with Leo, and they calmly relaxed.

I shoved past them, and made my way to my room with my Chick~fil~a.

I slammed the door closed, and locked it. I ate my sandwich, and drank the rest of my drink.

I walked down the stairs, prepared to throw my food away and run.

Recently, the men have been so much more aggravating in a protective and lust-filled way. It's been aggravating for me. It's like they're using me for pleasure. Not that I didn't enjoy it.

I do too, commented Uri.

I smiled, and laughed mentally. Uri joined in with me. If I had to say something about Uri, I would say that I would do anything for her by now.

I shouted to the guys that I was going for a run, and they could come if they wanted. But there was no answer.

I shrugged, and made my way outside. As I ran into the deep forest behind my house, I changed mid-step into my white and black-speckled wolf. I raced through the woods, feeling my muscles in my wolf form stretch out. I felt the forest underneath my paws, and it excited me.

I let Uri take over for her stretch, and went back into Uri's mind.

I wonder what the guys are doing, I told her.

I have no idea, she replied.

Do you think they know where we went?

Who cares? They've been overprotective and it's even been getting on my nerves. Plus, we'll be back soon enough.

I considered Uri's words, and decided to keep running.

_

After a long run, I turned to make my way back.

Halfway through my path, a familiar smell hit my nose. A smell of pine and apples. What is that?

Suddenly, a large black black shape barreled from the trees, and collided with me. I yelped, and tumbled to my side. The large wolf pinned me down gently but roughly. I looked up at the wolf, and noticed he had the same smell as Leo. Leo.

Thats who that is, I thought.

Yup, agreed Uri.

Four more shapes appeared behind Leo, and I recognized them as Mason, Luca, Anthony, and Dylan.

They all had anger radiating off of them. I gulped in fear.

What the hell did I do now?

The five boys dragged me back to the house. Them growling, and me whining. Once we got to the house, Dylan pinned me under his wolf. "Shift," he growled through the mind-link. I whined, and tried to shake him off of me, but he only pinned me tighter, and licked the sides of my nick, nuzzling my shoulder in the process.

"Shift," he said gently, and I did.

I shifted under his wolf, and covered my body. I eyed the wolves, and they all stared back at me hungrily. I glanced around at the lust-filled gazes, and blushed. I hid my face, as the boys shifted, and put on some jeans they had nearby. Dylan threw me a shirt, which I took greatfully.

Once I put the shirt on, and stood with the support of the wall, Leo slammed his arm into the wall on my left side, and Mason's arm on my right. They growled lustfully and angrily at me. I growled back, rage taking over.

"What?" I snapped, glaring at them.

"Where were you? Don't you dare leave this house without one of us with you!" Shouted Anthony from behind Mason. I glared at him.

"I did tell you. Before I left I said I was heading out and asked if you wanted to come but nobody said anything! And that's bull. I can do whatever I want! You don't have full control over me!" I snapped at him. His eyes darkened, and he stepped closer. A rush of fear overcame me, and I pressed my body into the wall. Mason looked at me darkly.

"Don't do that again. You worried us. Next time, come to our rooms. Or, better yet, don't leave at all." His voice almost sounded like he was begging.

I growled. "No. I am going out when I want, got that?!"

I moved past both boys, and stomped up to my room. I slammed my bedroom door closed, and locked it. I hopped on my bed, still steaming.

By the time I was done steaming, and the knocks and bangs and pleads from the boys to unlock the door faded, I was tired. I closed my eyes sleepily, and laid my head on my pillows, just as darkness took over.

P.O.V.

Shes so innocent when she sleeps. It's almost alluring. To her boys, at least. But I don't fall for things like that. She is my prey. That is all. I will take her from her boys, and kill her in front of them. That's the least I can do for revenge. After all, these boys are the Blood Brothers. The most ruthless pair of rogues to be known. They've taken down entire packs, even the alphas. They're known as the power houses, and now that they've got a weakness, I plan to make them regret ever getting near me and my deceased pack. Now all that's left is me and a few strong members.

Get ready brothers, because a war is coming.

This should be fun.

(Thank y'all so much for reading this chapter! Your support is so awesome to me, and I love you guys so much!)

Is This War?

Mavis

    I woke up the next morning, still groggy, and pissed, but ready to go for a run.

A run sounds nice, Uri added.

I smiled to myself, shaking my head in amusement.

I stripped from my pajamas, and stepped into the shower. I turned the water on warm, and began to scrub down my body. I cleaned up my hair, and stepped out. I always hated the feeling of being dirty.

I wrapped a towel around my hair, and dried off my body. I put on a pair of skinny jeans and put on a purple tank-top.

I made my way downstairs, ready to get out of the house. I sat down in the kitchen, grabbed a fudge pop-tart, and ate it hungrily. Stupid chocolate cravings. I'm not even on my period.

I finished the pop-tart, and moved to the living room, still a bit shocked at the silence. It was completely quiet - still. It was kind of nerve-wracking.

I decided to check up on the guys. I moved upstairs, and turned left. I moved down the hallway, and stopped after the second door. I didn't bother to knock, I didn't see why I had to, and walked in. Mason was asleep on a dark brown bed. Dark brown sheets covered his bed frame, and the walls were painted a beige. It was a strange room, honestly, while the furniture was a deep dark brown.

I smiled softly, and backed out of the room, slowly closing the door behind me.

I went to Luca, Dylan, and Anthony's room. All that was left was Leo's room.

I moved to the final bedroom, and opened it slowly. The room was painted black, with silver furniture and bed frame. The comforter was a black colour, and the carpet was black as well. It was a strange mix. I didn't see Leo's shape immediately, so I closed the door silently, and moved farther into the room.

Once I saw next to the bed, I easily saw Leo's form, and sighed silently in relief. My mates are safe.

I turned, ready to leave, but an arm latched onto me first. I turned in a flash, to see Leo's black hardened eyes glaring at me. I sucked in a breath, fear coursing through me. He growled possessively.

I let out a whimper, which caused Leo's eyes to soften. He jerked me into his bed, and spooned into my back. He burried his face into my neck, kissing the spot that connected my throat to my shoulder. I let out a small moan, which caused him growl lower. He pressed his body tighter to mine, and nibbled on my ear, his tiredness long gone.

"You're mine today," he whispered in my ear, causing me to shudder.

The door suddenly slammed open, and Dylan stormed in, his eyes filled with rage. He grabbed my arm, and roughly jerked me from Leo's grip.

Leo let out a roar, and hopped off the bed, only in his boxers. Dylan pushed me behind him protectively, and snarled back at him.

"What the hell are you doing?! She was mine!" Leo howled in rage and frustration.

"She was mine for tonight, but I didn't get her! It's not your turn! Don't mess with me right now. She's mine," Dylan snarled back. Leo let out a howl, and bent down to pounce on Dylan. I let out a whimper. I didn't want them fighting just to get hurt.

The door was shoved open once again, revealing Mason and Luca. Anthony stormed past them both. They all seemed tired, and completely pissed off.

"WILL YOU BOTH CALM DOWN?!" He shouted, causing me to flinch.

Strong arms wrapped around my waist, and I felt Luca cuddling up to me. I looked up at him, to see him smiling softly at me. I gave him a grateful smile, and turned back to the boys.

They all seemed to be bickering about something. Nothing too serious at this point. I sighed into Luca's embrace, and he let out a low chuckle. He pulled me tighter to him, and kissed my lips softly. His lips were gentle and warm, and I smiled into the kiss. He pulled back sharply, his beautiful blue eyes going black. I giggled, excited at the effect I had on him. On them all.

Thats when a loud knock - no, a bang - came from the front door. All of the guys immediately went silent. Thy all glanced at each other nervously.

I sighed at their behavior, and made my way out of Luca's arms, and went downstairs. I made my way to the door, the guys soon following after me.

I opened the door, to see a strange man there. But his scent was familiar.

Werewolf.

Uri agreed, her silent snarled heading in the stranger's direction. The stranger smirked. The guys growled. I glanced at them, confused at their behavior.

"Hello Blood Brothers. Good to see you again. And with your mate." He smirked. Leo growled lower. Anthony grabbed my hand, and pulled me to his chest. He picked me up, and I wrapped my legs around his waist. He wrapped his arms around me protectively. I burried my face into his neck. I felt someone stand in front of us. Scuffling and grunts were heard. Then cracks and fists colliding with flesh. I closed my eyes, and snuggled deeper into Anthony, who held me tighter. I smiled. Suddenly, the sounds stopped, but there was heavy breathing.

"Dont think this is over," the stranger's voice rang out. "This is just the beginning. And you better watch over your mate. She won't last too long otherwise." Another snarl rang out. It sounded like Mason.

I whimpered, fear overtaking me. He was going to kill me? Why?

I don't know, Uri whimpered. She hadn't spoken in a while, so I was glad to hear her voice.

I could hear someone being pushed, and the door was slammed shut. I turned my head to the guys, to see them all looking pissed. I raised my hand, and briefly touched each of their faces gently. They all seemed to calm down, and look at me.

"It's fine," I murmured reassuringly.

"It isn't fine," Leo snapped.

"This is war."

(Thank y'all for reading this chapter! I know I haven't published lately, but I appreciate your reads and support so much! Until the next chapter, see ya guys!)

His Return

WARNING - This chapter contains violent language.

1 Week Later

Mavis

Ever since that werewolf threatened us at our own doorstep, the guys have kept me locked down. It's like a prison now. Except they were all gentle with me. But if I get one more scolding speech for suggesting to go out, I will rip them all a new one about this. Even Uri is pissed.

"For the last time, you are not going out!" Mason slammed his fist against the long kitchen table that somehow had enough chairs to sit all six of us whenever we used it. Which was never. I fumed silently, rage overtaking me. *We should show him his place. He's our mate, not our master,* Uri howled, ready to come out. I felt a strong, warm hand wrap around mine comfortingly, and I glanced over at Anthony.

He gave me a small smile. *"Remember, we're all just scared for your safety. We love you, and we don't want anyone getting you,"* he mind-linked me. Uri sighed dreamily, instantly calming down. I sighed in exasperation, and nodded my head. I glanced back at Mason, who was silently fuming, while staring at Anthony's hand.

I stood up, and glared at Mason. "YOU listen to ME. Got that? I'm going out with or without your consent. It's been a week Mason. A fucking week. I'm not staying here any longer. Got me?" I growled. Mason looked shocked.

Since we had to pay for food, water bills, electric bills, and everything else, Leo, Luca, and Dylan all worked. Which left Anthony, Mason, and me at home. Which meant I had to deal with their period-fits. I shouldn't have to. They're guys. When one snapped at me, the other comforted me. And vise-versa. And I'm tired of it.

"You are not leaving this house. You're mine! Ours, I mean," Mason added, after Anthony let out a low snarl. I tried to not let out a laugh.

Thankfully, it stayed in.

"I'm going out. Now you all can either come with me and follow. Or you can stay and watch me leave." I turned, and stalked up to my room.

I closed the door, and locked it to be safe. I changed into a red crop-top, and a pair of dark high-waisted skinny jeans. I slipped on a pair of white high top converse.

I left my hair as it, and let it fall down into its long naturally ribbon-like curls on my back. It added to my natural beauty. Or at least that's what I've heard.

I then opened my make-up bag, and applied some eye shadow, eyeliner, making sure to style it as a cat-eye, added some mascara, blush, concealer on my scars, but there were hardly any on my face anymore somehow, and added blood-red lipstick, making my lips look bold. I knew the guys would go crazy protective over my looks, but why not get some revenge while I can? I giggled evilly to myself, and Uri joined in.

I opened my door, after checking my phone. It's now 3 pm. My goodness I spent two hours in my room.

I made my way downstairs, to see all of the guys there. They sat on the two black leather couches in the living room, facing the 75 inch flat screen tv. Of course, I thought, watching the football game behind them.

They seemed to all sense my presence, and they all turned. When they all saw me, their eyes darkened, showing their wolves were in control. I suppressed a shiver. Uri howled in joy at the attention she was getting from her mates. She seemed to be talking to the male wolves, Griffin, River, Alcoy, Rydis, and Islo.

Griffin was Leo's wolf, and he was constantly dominate in every situation. Not to say the other guys weren't excessively, but Griffin topped the cake.

River was Dylan's wolf. Surprisingly, River was protective, and never let anyone, male or female, within a three meter radius of me. It was cute to watch him pout when I scolded him. He would never yell at me, which made it even funnier.

Alcoy was Mason's wolf. He was a big sweetheart. He always stuck to my side like a love-struck puppy. He would always cuddle into me, and purr into my neck. The others always growled whenever Alcoy was cuddling with me, which led to him snarling at them. Whenever one of the guy's wolf came out, all of the other wolves followed. They were always together. The guys told me it was because they were so close.

Rydis was Anthony's wolf. He was the lustful one of the group. He would always shove Alcoy away from me, and mark his scent all over me, making the others keep him farthest from me. I always laughed whenever I saw them all.

Islo was obviously Luca's wolf. He was the funny, optimistic wolf, who always supported me. He was the least dominate and controlling, which didn't say much. He was annoying at least. These boys need help.

They all growled at my outfit, which I smirked at. I flicked my hand to say bye, and stalked out of the door, my hips swaying. A few steps out of the door, I felt a pair of hands grip my waist, and a seductive purr came from my right side. Rydis appeared next to me, his hands still on my waist, and he nibbled on my right earlobe, his eyes twinkling with desire. I shivered, my heart speeding up. Rydis grinned knowingly, before he was jerked away from me by Griffin, who was snarling at Rydis. Rydis let out a smug smile, before turning back to me. I rolled my eyes and continued down the driveway we had. I managed to grab the keys to the one of the four cars we had while I was in the living room. Secretly, the guys were loaded, but they only used that money for me, which annoyed me.

I got inside my favorite car, and hopped in. I didn't give a shit whether the guys hopped in or not. I was getting the hell outta here.

Just as I was about to close the front door, a hand stopped me, and arms curled around my waist. I heard the doors on the car being opened, and four of the guys sat inside. I recognized the now in-control guys, Dylan, Leo, Anthony, and Mason sitting inside. I turned, to see Luca holding my waist.

He lifted me up somehow, and sat down in my place, setting me now on his lap. I glared down at him, and he smirked mischievously, and waggled his eyebrows. I rolled my eyes, and moved to the other side, plopping myself onto Leo's lap.

Leo wrapped his arm around my waist possessively. He watches the guys smugly, and turned me to face him. I sighed in annoyance, ignoring Luca's grumbles, and faced Leo.

He grabbed my face gently with one hand, and pressed his lips to mine. He held me close, and I felt the car move faster than normal. Uri cheered at Leo's kiss, while she seemed to be chatting with Griffin. I smiled wickedly, and kissed him back, before pulling away, and resting my back to his chest, enjoying the rest of the ride, while the other guys glared at Leo, who seemed to be holding me tighter to him now. He's gonna kill me soon with the pressure.

_

We pulled up to the mall. As soon as Luca turned off the car, I sprang out as if I was a bat from hell.

The guys followed after me, each one chuckling at me. When Leo got out, he seemed pissed off, but calmed when I held his hand. However, the guys shut up as soon as I did.

We went shopping, me looking at things, them offering to buy it, and me rejecting them immediately. That went on for a while, as well as the occasional single guy stupid enough to be staring at me hungrily. One of the guys, usually Anthony, handles them. I laughed at their obvious jealousy, before continuing on.

But the whole time at the mall, I felt the chills as if I was being watched. I constantly glanced around without attracting the attention of the guys, but I found nobody there. But the feeling never stopped. I shivered, before continuing.

_

After a few hours of 'shopping', I suggested we all go out for a run in the forest. The guys agreed, ready to let their wolves free.

We made our way into the forest, stripped in separate spots, and we all morphed. I felt my bones snap, but it happened so fast I felt no pain. When I finished, I stretched out my paws, and made my way to the guys.

We sprinted into the forest. I let Uri take the lead, as the guys did with their wolves. I closed my eyes, knowing Uri was in control, and relaxed.

Uri suddenly went back inside me, forcing me to take control. Uri was whimpering, which confused me. After asking her what's wrong, and her refusing to tell me, I glanced around, and stopped running. The guys, still with their wolves in control, stopped, and noticed I was back in my body. They came back to me, and comforted my now shaking body.

Something was wrong.

Suddenly, a twig snapped. We all jerked our heads in that direction. The guys formed a circle around me, watching the woods from their spot. Each of their pelts were touching mine, which helped them relax, knowing I was there.

Wolves came out from the forest all around us. There were so many. Every wolf had black pelts, and they walked in rows surrounding us. I swallowed nervously, and glanced around me. The guys snarled louder. I jerked my head at a chuckle. I let out a sharp breath, as the infamous Alessandro and the school bad-boy Jesse stood there. Both were in their human forms, and they were standing at the head of the wolves. There was no way! Alessandro is dead! I saw him die! Unless he healed.

No.

Fuck.

I forgot.

He's a vampire, of course he healed. He didn't die. His throat was sliced, which couldn't kill him.

Oh no.

Defeat

Warning - This chapter contains violent language

Mavis

Alessandro chuckled which seemed to ring out through the forest. I shivered, letting fear lance through my heart.

Why is he back? Of all things he had to be a vampire, I thought.

Alessandro's eyes seemed to swallow me up as he completely ignored the other guys. Uri let out a low snarl followed by a sharp whine. I couldn't help but let my own out as well.

Alessandro frowned at the sound and suddenly appeared in front of me, past Griffin at my front. I let out a louder whimper as Griffin whipped around.

Just as Griffin turned, Jesse launched forward, turning into his own black furred and golden eyed wolf.

He's a wolf too?

Alessandro gently grabbed my chin, demanding my attention. The other guys turned and Alessandro snapped his fingers. The other black wolves surged forward. The guys had to choice but to turn back around and defend themselves. I let out a pathetic sob, tears filling my eyes at the violent sight.

I'm defenseless.

That's next to the worst thing possible at this moment.

Alessandro let out a low chuckle and bent down next to me. He was at least a foot taller than me, which gave him a strong intimidating look. His cyan eyes met mine and I shivered in disguist.

Alesaandro's eyes turned sad.

"Baby, I'm so sorry I ever hit you. I hope you forgive me. I promise I'll never do that again. I learned after my punishment of you being away from me. I love you, little flower. I won't ever let you leave me again," he whispered in my ear before nibbling on the outer shell gently. I grit my teeth angrily and jerk my head away from his teeth. It somehow seemed to surprise him.

He turned to face me. Shock was on his features, which melted into a sly smirk.

"You've always caught me off guard. My beautiful flower, you're so defiant. Don't worry, I'll fix that about you. I love this about you, but you'll learn with my new ways of punishments for only you," he purred, which made bile rise up my throat.

At this point my men were being held down. They were still in their wolf forms. I could see Alcoy trying his best to fight off the eight wolves holding him down, but he could no longer move. My men were drained. I flushed. We were defeated. Jesse's wolf stood from his spot next to Griffin's limp body and came next to me. I knew Griffin was still alive. I saw his chest moving up and down slowly.

I managed a silent sigh in relief and glanced back at Jesse in pure hatred. These two did this. I can't believe this!

Jesse's wolf purred at the sight of me as he came up to me. I snarled at him, which made Jesse's wolf somehow frown, so he pressed his side against me. Jesse was the size of a pony at least, which made him over twice as large as my size. I watched him warily.

Werewolves had always been larger than normal wolves. I'm not talking Twilight huge, but almost that size.

Jesse's wolf walked around me, and I knew he was trying to put his scent on me. Alessandro hissed at Jesse's wolf, who growled back at him before retreating, satisfied.

"Mutts," Alessandro hissed before grabbing my wrist and picking me up by the waist. I yelped in shock, which caused snarls to come from the forms of my large and intimidating men. Their whining at me was clear now as I turned to them, tears shining in my eyes.

My boys, no!

Alessandro placed me on the back of now in-control Jesse, who growled at me in warning to hold onto his fur. I let out a sigh of defeat. I know I couldn't fight against his strength. I can't believe this is happening, I thought. Uri agreed. I could tell she was talking to the guys. I don't know what about, but I hope it's about an escape.

I held on to Jesse's fur lightly, trying my best not to touch him. Just as Jesse was about to start running, I tumbled off and landed lightly on my toes. I turned and started sprinting to Islo who was closest to me. I could hear shouts behind me but I didn't care. I shifted mid-run and I felt the shouts stop for a split second before continuing. I stopped at Islo and tore the wolves off of him, just as Jesse came.

River

It's hard to watch your loving, caring mate being taken from you right in front of your eyes. The worst part is the fact that she's screaming for you to help while sobbing. My blood was boiling at this point. Every instinct, including Dylan himself, was screaming at me to protect her. Rip those men away from her and protect her. Telling me that she's only safe in my arms.

Like I didn't know that, I scoffed.

Just as Alessandro put Mavis on Jesse's back for Jesse to take off, Mavis hopped off. I felt pride and relief swell through me. That's my girl.

She runs to Islo, causing jealousy to course through me. Of all wolves, why did it have to be Islo? Why wasn't it me?

She tore the wolves off of him, and my hope grew. It deflated right when Jesse got to her. Even though she was in her own beautiful wolf form, she was at least a head and a half smaller than Jesse. She stood no chance. Islo tore the rest of the wolves off of him and leapt at Jesse. Alessandro tackled Islo before he could get to Jesse and punched Islo in the jaw, instantly knocking him out. Mavis screamed while I let out a roar of pure fury, my sight tinging with red. Griffin and Rydis joined in, however Alcoy could barely make a sound due to the pressure of the other wolves.

Jesse picked up the now defeated petite frame of my mate in his jaws, gentler than I thought possible and started to carry her away from us.

I howled in pain. I didn't want to be away from my mate. What would they do to her? I saw the scars along her beautiful skin. Alessandro deserves to fucking die! I can't believe Anthony didn't kill him to begin with.

That idiot!

I watched my mate being carried away by the most infuriating wolf known.

We all knew Jesse was interested in Mavis and wanted to take her as his mate. We always protected her from him, thankfully, but now we have no control over what he does. He could take her from us. Claim her. Make her his. It hurts to even think about that. My girl with that...that...monster. Just as Jesse disappeared into the distance with Alessandro, all I could think was..

My mate....no.

Mavis

Jesse sat my wolf body on a soft bed inside the vampire and now werewolf mansion. I quickly moved from the other wolf, who sighed and climbed onto the bed. The bed freaked while somehow managing to hold his weight. The large wolf curled himself around me, preventing me from moving or even talking. I whined, showing my fear. Jesse merely chuckled, his wolf form rumbling in amusement.

He dug his nose into my fur and inhaled deeply. He growled when he caught the scent of my mates on me. I smiled smugly, which seemed to enfuriate him even more. He snarled viciously and wrapped himself tighter around me. I whined once more, tilting my neck back and showing my submission. I had no choice, he was hurting me!

Jesse relaxed and drew his rough tongue over my ruffled fur, like a father would to his pup. I couldn't help but feel a small pit of warmth in my stomach at his comforting actions. I've always wanted a father.

I was abandoned on my own since I was seven, and the guys' families took me in. I was always grateful. But it wasn't the same. Jesse purred into my fur and I soon closed my eyes, letting sleep take over. I didn't care where I was, I was just too tired. I want my boys. I want my mates.

Where are they?

Jesse

She was so beautiful. I had never seen such an innocent she-wolf before. Even as a human, she had all of my attention.

And all of my affection.

When we first met, she was the only girl that had snapped at me. I had never been so mesmerized. She had my heart ever since that first day. She just never knew.

She has my heart as well, added Rhen my wolf. She even had my wolf hooked.

Not every wolf has a mate. Only a rare few. One in every hundred thousands weres get true mates. Which means only a handful of weres in history have had true mates. So she is just as rightfully mine as she is to those rogues!

She'll love my power over theirs. I'm an alpha, after all.

Thats why I made the deal to merge my pack with Alessandro's group. I plan on taking her from Alessandro when he least expects it. I'll just have to be clever. She's rightfully mine, after all.

I loved her since our first meeting. An accidental one, at that.

But those bastards thought that they could just take her from me? Never. I'll have to punish them for that.

She was mine first. I loved her first. Their claim means nothing. I'll take her from them. I'll even make them watch her fall for me and only me. I'll mark her, go through every step. Claim her.

And make her mine.

Unmarked

Mavis

The first thing I felt when I woke up was soft fur presssed against mine.

I could feel my paws and tail, too. I must still be in wolf form.

Sunlight from an unknown source filtered through my lazily closed lids, forcing them open. I groaned. I didn't want to get up yet. This warmth was so comforting.

Out of instinct, I cuddled closer to the unknown source. I snuggled my muzzle into it's fur. The unknown source seemed to rumble, which confused me.

Out of, yet again, instinct, I raised my head quickly. I was met with beautiful golden eyes that seemed to melt my heart.

Jesse's eyes.

I yelped, and sprang from the bed I was resting in. Jesse turned his head to where I was, and followed after me, growling softly at my lack of warmth.

I yelped in fear, and scrambled away from him once he got closer. He snarled, and bounded forward, black pelt rippling, and trapped me against the wall. He leaned down from his giant height, and faced my petite frame. He let out a soft rumble out of humor, and nuzzled his nose into my neck comfortingly.

I couldn't help the small unexplainable noise that came from my throat. Jesse jerked back, the smell of sexual desire burning from him. I felt fear ripple throughout me. Jesse let out a low, possessive growl. He moved closer somehow, and pressed himself closer to me. His eyes were pitch black, letting me know his wolf took over.

He shifted back into his human body, showing me too much bare skin. He turned, and made his way towards the closet. He came out with boxers and jeans. He shoved on the pair of boxers and slipped on the jeans, and came back to me. He pinned me down, but I seemed frozen to the spot. He growled lustfully.

"Shift," he ordered in an alpha tone, and I had no choice but to do as he said.

As I shifted, I held my parts with my hands, covering them. Jesse radiated even more sexual desire. He picked me up, ignoring my hands, and tossed me on the bed. He climbed on top of me. I seemed to gain control of my body at that moment, and opened my mouth to scream.

Unfortunately, Jesse was faster.

He slammed a hand over my mouth, which caused tears to form in my eyes. Jesse's eyes softened, and his grip loosened slightly, not enough so I could escape, but enough to take the pain away.

He grabbed a small vial of a pink liquid, which seemed to glow. He opened the small lid, and gripped my chin gently. He moved my head back, exposing my neck, and my marks. He gently poured a small amount on one of the marks on my neck.

Leo's mark.

The pink liquid absorbed into the mark, and a stabbing pain filled the area there. I screamed, and threw my head back. Thousands of needles seemed to be shoving their way into that one spot endlessly.

I knew that Leo's mark was disappearing, I could tell. By the time the mark was gone, I was tired, the pain was excruciating, and I could barely take it.

He then turned to my collar bone.

Dylan, I thought.

He dumped the potion on the rest of the marks all at once. I had never felt anything so painful. Fire splashed through my veins, moving so slowly, the pain carried its way through my system. Jesse held me the whole time, murmuring sweet-nothings to me.

Why? Why is he doing this? And why is he holding me?

I could tell I was unmarked by the end of he pain, and that just made the loneliness worse. It hurt so much, my mates, gone.

Jesse smiled, he seemed too happy about all of this. He grabbed both of my weak arms, and pinned them over my head. I was too tired to do anything. I could feel Jesse remove his hand from my mouth and grab my chin. I saw a blurry figure that had dark hair and molten gold eyes come closer, these white things coming from his mouth.

I could feel this sharp pain in my neck. It felt like what a marking would feel like, but I wouldn't know. I could feel something warm and wet run over where the sharp pain was. Then, a warm body appeared by my side on the bed. I didn't see any blurry figure in front of me, so I'm guessing the guy moved to my side. I could feel his arms wrap around me, pinning me to him. I felt a vibration in my neck, where his mouth was.

Right as darkness took over, I could hear,

"You are mine now. All mine."

Mason

All I felt was pain and the loss of my mate.

I was chained to a wall of concrete, my other three sides having been made of metal bars. To my right was Anthony, and to my left was Luca. To say this wasn't cliché would have been an understatement.

After Mavis was taken from us, we had been dragged to the vampire and werewolf mansion, and locked up here. It's been at least two days, and all I could feel was the empty space where my mate should be. I'm upset at what they could be doing.

No, I'm pissed.

I was deep in thought, when a sharp pain jabbed through my chest. My collar bone felt as if a dagger had been shoved there, taken out, then changed with a silver dagger, and stabbed back inside, even deeper. I howled out in pain, joining the guys in their own agonizing yelps. The guards outside our cell just smirked. The one on the left leaned to the one on the right, and whispered loud enough for us to hear, and obviously in a mocking tone.

"I bet Alpha Jesse has finished unmarking his mate, our Luna, Mavis. I hear that he planned on unmarking her and marking her as his own today. I bet he'll even try to get her round with his pups soon after." The second one smirked and followed after.

"Yeah, and I hear that he's taking her back to the pack house, and claiming her."

Through the pain, anger slammed throughout me. My mate has been taken from me?!

I let out a howl of anguish, and felt rage brimming from every cell of my body. My poor angel must be suffering. The thought of my little mate in that devil's arms is enough to make me snap the chains holding me back, and lunge at the unsuspecting guards. The other guys seemed to mimic my movement, and let out snarls. The guards tried their best, but were no match.

I stood from the two crippled bodies, and the pools of blood that circled the guys and my feet, and glared at the other prisoners, who seemed to be watching us in awe.

I raised my voice to the prisoners.

"We are the Blood Brothers, the most well-known rogues of all time. Our mate is here, and we are going to rescue her. Are you in or out?"

The prisoners all seemed to stiffen with fear or curiosity. There wasn't a single soul out there that didn't know of the Blood Brothers. We're known for our ruthless attacks on packs that threaten us or others that we care about. We're known as heroes to pack-less wolves. Some of the prisoners here seemed to relax, even smile a bit.

My eyes gleamed in blood-hunger, and the prisoners glanced at each other warily, before turning back to me.

They nodded, and I smiled ruefully.

Leo flicked his hand, and we all went forward. We slashed open the locks, and the rogues and prisoners tumbled out.

I turned to the stairs, where the unsuspecting guards were.

"Let's go get out mate back!" Howled Leo, and we all followed after him, as he charged through the prison.

We're coming, little mate. Just hold on.

(Hey guys! Thank you guys so much for reading this chapter. I love you guys so much and thank you all for all of the support! Until the next chapter guys (who knows when that will be) I'll see y'all later!)

Why Did This Happen?

I want to apologize in advance if anyone has had any experience or incident with rape, molestation, or any kind of sexual cruelty in their life. I apologize in advance. Please don't be offended with anything in this chapter, but it's a part of the story so I need to put it in. Thank you guys and enjoy the chapter!

Mavis

When I came to, all I saw was black. Maybe that was because I was facing the ceiling.

Idiot, Uri muttered.

Shut up.

I slowly widened my eyes to try to wake up, or at least remember something. A small ache came from the corner of my neck, where my shoulder meets it. I couldn't help but stick my arm up to rub at it. When I pressed my hand to my neck, I could feel a small bump there. No, two small bumps. Followed by another two inside and diagonal to each of the top bumps. It was a mark.

A tingle of pleasure shot through me, making me hold back a moan. But something felt wrong. I moved my hand to my forearm, to feel for Luca's mark, only to come up empty handed. I started to panic.

That's when I felt the arms around me. They felt warm, comforting. But I could feel a sense of dread where that arm came in contact with my skin. I hated the feeling just as much as I loved it. This isn't Mason's, Leo's, Luca's, Anthony's, or Dylan's.

No.

I turned around slowly.

Resting behind me, his body barely away from mine, was Jesse. I bit back a scream.

Fear coursed through my veins, as everything came back to me. He removed their marks. I felt tears pool in my eyes. Sadness flowed through my veins. All of the memories I had with the guys. The feelings, the moments, the kisses, the touches. He took them.

He took everything from me.

I could feel my Uri sadly turn towards Jesse and his wolf, and communicate with them. I was sad too. He forced his mark onto us, thus changing fate and making us his mate. It was one of the worst things you could do if you still have a living mate. It's truly awful. I could feel hate running through my blood, pumping it faster. As if on cue, Jesse's golden eyes opened. When he saw me, a smile lit up his features. And he tightened his muscled arms, pulling me closer to him. I whimpered, fear rising up through me. This man could do anything he wanted, and I wouldn't be able to stop him. He was just too strong.

Jesse's eyes softened, and he raises one hand, and tucked a lock of my hair behind my ear, and leaned forward to kiss my forehead. I cringed back in disguist, which seemed to piss him off. He flipped me suddenly, and pinned my arms down on the bed, resting above me. A look of lust passed through his eyes, and I could scent strong sexual desire in the room. Jesse leaned close to my ear. "You are mine now, mate. Mine to do anything with. I love you. You are so beautiful. You don't understand how much I want to touch you and claim you," he whispered seductively, causing chills to force their way onto my skin.

I growled, and ripped my arms from his grip. "You do NOT own me. Got it? I am my own person. You are nothing to me. My mates are my boys. You are not them," I hissed.

Shouldn't have done that.

Jesse let out a ferocious roar. It seemed to shake the whole room, making the furniture vibrate.

He grabbed my arms again, and pinned them above my head, he grabbed both wrists tightly with one hand, securing them. I screamed, fear shaking me to my core. Jesse leaned down, and started to gently nibble on his mark, forcing me to let out a small whine. I couldn't help it. It was the forced mate bond.

Jesse smiled, obviously pleased, before he moved one arm down out of my sight. I had no idea what he was doing. Fear coursed through me once again as the sound of a zipper rang throughout the room. I screamed once again, only to be stopped short by Jesse's mouth.

THIS IS WHERE THE RATED R SECTION STARTS IF YOU DON'T WANT TO READ THEN SKIP AHEAD

I could feel him rip off my shorts, then underwear, and I started to kick anything I could. Jesse grunted as I landed one to his stomach somehow, before moving faster. I could feel his member pressed against my entrance, and I screamed once more, tears pressed against my eyelids, and fell down my face. Uri whined, trying her best to get Jesse's wolf to stop Jesse.

But it didn't work.

THIS IS WHERE IT GETS NASTY SO SKIP AHEAD IF YOU DON'T WANT TO READ!!!!

Jesse shoved deep inside of me in one thrust, breaking my virgin barrier and causing me to scream louder and tears to form. Jesse's mouth didn't stop the volume.

Jesse pulled out, while releasing my lips from his, and I could feel the blood leaking out of my entrance. Tears fell down my face. I can't believe he took my virginity. He's raping me.

Uri let out a pitiful howl, no longer talking to Rhen, Jesse's wolf.

"STOP IT!" I screamed, pain coursing throughout me, quickly followed by pleasure. Jesse looked into my eyes, his close-to-black eyes filled with love and pleasure.

"Why would I stop? You love this. I'll fully claim you and we can do this every day, I can make you round with my pups, and fill you with my offspring," he growled out possessively, and I felt more tears fall down my face. He took what I wanted to give my boys. He took everything I had to give. He's a monster. He doesn't love me.

Jesse started to pump inside of me, making the pleasure fill me forcefully. But I didn't like it. I hated it.

Jesse kept going, his thrusts getting longer and harsher, before releasing inside of me, giving me the chance of being pregnant. I let the sobs rack through my body. The thought of being a mother to this monster's children gave me chills of fear.

He slowed his movement, but he kept pumping inside. Pulling out. Pushing in. That's how the pattern went. He groaned in complete pleasure, before releasing once more. I didn't cum once. I was disgusted.

RATED R MOMENT ENDS HERE

The door banged open suddenly, revealing the five men I've been waiting for. My boys stormed through the room. They all froze when they saw Jesse. Leo roared, followed by Anthony, and the two boys ripped Jesse from me, causing me to sob in relief. I could feel the small tears falling down my cheeks. Luca and Mason came up to me. Mason wrapped me in a warm blanket that smelled of him and Dylan, and Luca held me to him, murmuring sweet things to me, while Anthony, Leo, and Dylan killed Jesse slowly.

I closed my eyes, and turned away. I can't believe this happened to me. Luca held me tighter, growling at the mark Jesse had, and the smell of him on me. I gripped Luca's shirt.

"Luca, take it away. Take the mark away," I begged, tears once again falling from my eyes. Luca's eyes darkened, befor she swiftly leaned down, and shoved his fangs into my neck over Jesse's mark.

I sighed in relief, feeling the bond between me and Jesse break. Leo marked me once again. He kissed me softly. I sighed, fear coursing through me at the feeling over my core. It was still burning.

The boys finished off Jesse, and surrounded me immediately.

They all snarled at the scent of Jesse on me. I had to calm them down.

They all took turns remarking me, not giving me the chance to rest. I was too dazed to remember who marked where.

When they finished, Anthony jerked me from Luca's grip, causing Luca to let out a low snarl and grab my arm, pulling me back to him.

"I was holding her. Give her back," Luca snapped.

"Take turns. She isn't just yours," argued Anthony. I grumbled, too tired to comment, as they carried me home, along with a few strangers I talked with on the way there.

Dylan

I could still smell him on her. It pissed off my wolf. I could tell he raped her. That caused me to rip Jesse's bloody carcass apart. I can never forgive myself for what happened to my mate. The trauma she's gone through. I can't believe myself.

But I won't ever let her go again.

She's back with us.

I wrapped my arms around her petite frame, pulling her closer to me on my bed in my bedroom. Tonight is my night with her, after all.

I kissed her head gently, listening to her soft breathing. I'm going to do everything I can to make sure she never has any more pain again.

My poor mate.

I'll protect you now.

HEY YAAAAALLL. I know two in one day I'm such a badass. Remember to C V O O M T M E E N

T

Hospitalized

Mavis

    I had always assumed the good things happened to the kind people, and the bad things happened to the evil people. I knew that there may have been a few bumps in the road for everyone, but I never thought once that that bump would be a wall.

A wall that couldn't be moved. It went as high as the sky, and even dug into the ground. It was solid iron.

What happens then?

I can say now that this is the most empty with emotions, at the same time as the most emotions I've ever envountered, that I've ever felt. But I can say this much:

In all words, all it can really put together is the fact that I'm scared. Terrified. Knowing that there wasn't just one life, one soul, one mind, one body. Not one heart. Not one heartbeat.

In the darkness, there were two.

Thump thump, thump thump. The beat of their heartbeats roared in the ears of a girl who knew nothing of the cruelty in the world. Nothing of having her own future. Nothing of getting married, having children, growing old with the ones she loved.

But all she knew, in that hazy darkness that was called unconsciousness, was that there wasn't one heartbeat. There was two.

She knew. She wasn't ready, but she didn't care. She wasn't going to give up because of who or what did this.

There was a baby inside of her, and she was keeping it. There was a baby inside of me, and I'm keeping it. Keeping the little mistake. But it wasn't a mistake. It doesn't have to know. I won't let it know.

I love this baby. So, so much.

Leo

It has been a day. Another day. A week. No response.

Nothing from my precious mate.

We all knew that she had been through hell. Fuck, you can still see it on her beautiful face in the hospital bed she was resting on. Her long wavy brown hair fell in messy clumps down her sides, or squished beneath her back, where it meets the bed. I sat on the small plastic chair in the room, Mason and Luca resting on the small couch next to me. Dylan and Anthony were sitting on the two chairs on the opposite sides of the room. We all looked like shit.

We haven't moved from this spot for hours, days. And I'm not planning on moving anytime soon. I don't give a damn waht the other guys do at this point, I'm just staying with my mate.

I could feel that she was okay in my heart, but that didn't stop the restless Griffin from howling in grief from the absence of his beautiful and petite mate. I can't eat, sleep, or even get up to use the bathroom without thinking about Mavis. Her beautiful smell, intoxicating beauty, angelic voice. She is all I can see now. She haunts my dreams, forcing me to stay awake. I wish I could hate her for it.

But I could never do that to her. I love her too much.

We would never leave her, Griffin snarled. I agreed mentally.

I glanced around the room. The alarm clock read 6:47 am. The guys all around me were the same as me. Conscious but not in their minds. They were all slowly going insane. As the leader, I could feel it. Deep inside my bones like a powerful urge to slam my fist into an innocent wall.

An accelerated beep, beep, beep startled me, causing me to snap my head so fast I almost had whiplash. I stared down the bed Mavis rested on, as her beautiful violet eyes slowly opened. I could feel my entire body shut down in relief. I let out a small growl, causing the other guys to glance at Mavis, then return their gaze back to her as they realized she was awake. Anthony stood up so fast his chair toppled over, while Luca and Dylan ran to Mavis's side instantly.

"Little mate, you've been out for a week. Are you okay? We'll never hurt you again. We killed Jesse for what he did. You're safe now," Mason rambled nervously, as he held a death grip with her small hand. I couldn't help but silently fume at his closeness with her.

I stood up, and shoved my way past Mason, bending down to softly kiss Mavis's sweet, soft lips. It took her a moment, but she slowly wrapped her thinner arms around me, causing me to growl in approval.

Snarls rang throughout the room, as I was ripped away from Mavis by a raging Anthony. I growled and snapped my teeth at him, which usually caused him to submit and apologize, but this time he merely glared back.

"Why the hell did you kiss her?!" Shouted Mason.

"Yeah! Why do you get her first? She's mine too!" Growled Luca, causing me to turn and snarl at him, making him flinch a little. I let out a menacing growl, forcing my friends to submit. A small whimper made me whip around, and instantly soften. Mavis was on the opposite side of the bed from where I saw, whining and showing her neck in submission. But for whatever reason she was holding on to her stomach. Maybe she was just hungry. It would be understandable.

I reached out for her, but growled when Dylan picked her up from the other side before I could touch her. She snuggled into his chest, making me let out another growl. Dylan's chest rumbled with laughter as her small head burried into his neck. He kissed her forehead lovingly, and he dug his nose into her neck. I stomped towards Dylan, grabbing her waist and pulled her from him. Dylan let go, startled. But when he saw me his eyes darkened. I forced Griffin back at his obvious challenge, and merely huffed at him. When I looked fown, I could tell my mate was tired. I wrapped her legs around me, and turned to the door.

"Let's take Mavis home, guys."

_

After checking Mavis out, signing medical forms, giving her a check-up, and driving home with four guys constantly fighting over who would hold Mavis, we finally got back to the house. I could tell Mavis was physically drained, so I set her in her bed in her bedroom, and rested next to her, pulling the covers over both of us, and engulfing her body with mine.

Once I felt her even breaths, I knew she was asleep. The door opened, and Luca stepped through, closing it silently. He rested on the bed behind Mavis, and silently wrapped his arms around her back. I raised my eyebrow, but didn't argue, as I slowly lowered my head on the pillow that was close to me, and slowly fell asleep.

(Hope y'all emjoyed the extra filler chapter! Love u guys so much!)

Announcement

Mavis

The first thing I could sense was the soft bedsheets that surrounded me, followed by two muscled bodies on either side of mine. I could feel the soft bed underneath my smooth skin.

I opened my tired eyes, to see my old bedroom. I sighed in relief. So it wasn't a dream. I could feel my body slowly relax. I glanced to my sides, to see Leo and Luca on either side of me, both had their arms wrapped around my body, Leo's on my chest, and Luca's on my stomach.

Their bodies pressed close to mine, which also squeezed my stomach. I internally growled. My motherly instincts kicked in. I shoved Leo away from my stomach while snarling. Both Leo and Luca jumped up in surprise, which caused them both to fall off the bed. I stifled a laugh, trying to still be pissed at them. I unconsciously wrapped my arms around my stomach protectively.

Leo and Luca's eyes trailed to my arms, which caused me to snap at them again, before I felt the bile rise up my throat. I suddenly slammed my hand to my mouth, feeling the vomit coming into my mouth, and sprinted into the bathroom. I vomited into the toilet, thankful I made it on time. I heaved constantly, while feeling soothing hands on my shoulders, and another pair pulling my hair behind me.

By the time I was done, I could sense all of the guys came into the room. I sighed, and rubbed my hand over my mouth, palm away, to get rid of the rest on the vomit. I could still taste it, which made me shiver in disguise. I moved away from Leo and Luca and began to clean and brush my teeth. I quickly spit out the mouthwash I had, and turned to the guys. Anthony was the first to hug me, then Dylan, and after him it was Mason. Leo and Luca hung back, since they already slept with me.

Mason carried me downstairs and sat me on one of the dining room chairs. I stared at the table, not wanting to say anything. I was awfully hungry though.

I knew I was pregnant, and even though it wasn't who I wanted to be, I'm still having Jesse's child. I don't care that it was from him, I wanted to keep it. I loved it. But how would the guys take it? Would they leave me? Would they think I was damaged goods? I'm keeping the baby regardless. I have to tell them. I have to. I have to. I have to.

It would be best, Uri added.

I stood up. All the guys' attention snapped to me. I took a deep breathe, and exploded.

"I have to tell you something," I squeaked. Dylan stood up, and moved behind me, rubbing my shoulders soothingly.

"You can tell us anything Mavis," Leo murmured. I nodded.

"I'm pregnant," I whispered so quietly, no human would have been able to hear.

Unfortunately, we aren't human.

It was silent for one split second, even Dylan's hands stopped, before everything exploded.

"WHO TOUCHED YOU?!" Leo shouted in pure rage.

"IT'S JESSE'S ISN'T IT?!" Added Anthony, who seemed to become sad along with pissed.

Dylan wrapped his hands around my shoulders, and pulled me flush against his body. Sparks raced through my body, causing me to shiver.

"What are you going to do with the baby?" He whispered angrily in my ear. All the guys seemed to hear him, and they stopped, and stared at me hungrily, waiting for my answer.

"I want to keep the baby. Not because of the father, but because this baby doesn't know anything. It doesn't know about it's father. It is innocent. For all it knows, Leo or Anthony is it's father," I said in one breath, which almost made me pass out.

Leo's eyes darkened, before he stormed out of the room, Anthony on his tail to calm him down. You could hear arguing upstairs, along with a door slamming. I flinched, sadness overtaking me. I felt three pairs of arms around me. I glanced up, to see Luca, Dylan, and Mason smiling sadly at me.

"I'm sure Leo just needs some time," Dylan purred.

"We don't like the fact that some other man's baby is inside of you, but we will get over it, and take care of that baby like it's our own," added Mason.

Luca burrowed his head into my neck, silently rubbing his mouth against his mark gently.

I sighed, before glancing at the stairs that led upstairs.

I hope Leo is okay.

Forgiveness

Mavis

It's been three days. You should understand that three days doesn't seem long, but when your mate is so close to you, yet so far, you want to be with them. It's killing me and Uri to not go out there and kiss them senseless.

Leo hasn't spoken a word to me, he hasn't even glanced my way since I announced my pregnancy. I can get his pissy mood because it's not his or his friends' baby. It's someone he hate's baby. I'm in no better mood about it, but Leo is really starting to piss me off.

Im the pregnant one in the relationship. He should be helping me like the other guys are. Not sitting in his room thinking about probably how much of a mistake I am. I'm so pissed off im ready to tear into his room and claw him in half. He doesn't have to carry the baby, hell, he has no idea what it's like to give birth. I don't either, but I will soon enough.

To say in pissed would be an understatement. If he wants to be a brat about it though, I won't stop him. I had my other mates that love and support me. But I can't help the pang of sadness that overcame me.

The boys weren't any happier than Leo, I wasn't stupid. I knew that much. But at least they hid it. I was thankful for that much.

I stalked into the kitchen, but I stopped short when I saw Leo. He was just sitting in the kitchen. Almost as if nothing had happened. I couldn't help the feeling of rage that overcame me.

He doesn't even acknowledge us, roared Uri.

I know! What an ass, I agreed.

I had to hold back the feeling of Uri surging forward. She wanted to claw Leo's eyes out at the same time as she wanted to curl up into him.

I cleared my throat bluntly, causing Leo's head to snap in my direction. His eyes narrowed into slits, anger at the same time as sadness flooded through his eyes. I've always been pretty good at reading peoples' emotions through their eyes. Leo surged forward from his chair. I jumped back from shock, and began to back away slowly. He stalked slowly towards me. Once he reached me, I couldn't help but take a cautious step back. He followed my steps. But I wasn't going to do the cliche thing like backing into the wall. No way. I stood in place, glaring at Leo with the same intensity as he did to me. It was like fire clashing with fire. Nothing good was coming from it. I felt him grab my arm roughly.

I squeaked in pain when his grip tightened. He bent down to my height, and whispered angrily in my ear, "I want that pup inside of you gone. I don't want to remember that mutt or anything about him, especially from you. I want my seed inside of you. I want to impregnate you. But instead you want to keep that mutt's baby? You are starting to piss me off with how protective of the baby you are." "That's not true! This little baby has nothing to do with it's father!" I argued back. Leo growled.

"I. Want. It. Gone," he whispered huskily, before nipping gently on my earlobe, forcing a loud moan to come from my lips. My eyes widened in shock.

This baby makes me even more sensitive, I suppose. He smiled in smug satisfaction, before moving back and lightly cupping my face with one hand. He leaned down once again, and gently kissed me on my lips, his kiss being rough but gentle. I couldn't help the sparks that ignited between us when he clashed his lips against mine.

I wrapped my arms around his neck, kissing him back slowly. He circled his arms around my waist, and pulled me to him possessively.

But after a little bit, we both needed air. He released me reluctantly. I stepped back, scared of being near him. The electric shock between us was hot enough to burn down the house at this point. I was beginning to wonder where my other boys went. They were home last time I checked.

He leaned down one last time, and murmured, "I forgive and love you, but that baby will never be loved by me." He stepped back once more, before stalking out of the kitchen, leaving me pretty much angry, speechless, and horny.

Of course, when I left the kicthen with a fudge pop tart, Anthony decided to make his appearance. He snuck up behind me, and wrapped his arms around my waist, and small baby bump, and pulled me gently to him. I dropped my pop tart. But it was long forgotten after a second. He nestled his nose into the crook of my neck, and inhaled deeply. He kissed my neck where his mark was deeply, and smiled when I closed my eyes and not my lip to hold back a moan.

Anthony gently pushed me back on the couch. I landed with a soft thud, and Anthony came on top of me, his forearms pinning me to the couch.

Anthony glanced into my eyes for permission, which I granted with a nod, before capturing my lips in a heated kiss.

WARNING - SEXUAL CONTENT AHEAD

TO SKIP THIS SCENE GO TO THE SIGN THAT SAYS SEXUAL CONTENT ENDED

Anthony pulled away from my lips, only to rip my shirt and shorts off roughly. I gasped in surprise, lust forming inside my lower stomach, and heat pooled between my thighs.

Anthony trailed kisses from my neck to his mark, causing me to moan out, and continued downward to my breasts, he gently wrapped one arm around to my back, where he unclasped my bra.

As he did, I felt a second pair of hands grip my thighs, and spread my legs apart. Anthony moved to the side to give the mystery figure room, and when I lifted my head, I could see it was Mason.

Mason ripped off my underwear hungrily. Once he got them off, he stared to stare at my part as if it was his first time seeing such a thing, before moving his fingers to my folds, and started rubbing gently, causing electric shocks to go through my body. I let out what seemed to be a mix between a whimper and a groan, as he started to stick a finger into my core, then a second one, before moving in and out deeply, thrusting deeper each time.

Anthony started to ran and massage my breasts, while suckling on one nipple, I let out another moan, as my core started to heat up more and more, and suddenly, a wave of pleasure ran through my body, as shudders crashed through me. I saw black for a few seconds, my eyes moving to the back of my head in pleasure. I rested my body against the now wet couch with my sweat, as I panted uncontrollably. My heartbeat was erratic, but I felt nothing but tiredness and pure pleasure.

My two men chuckled, before moving away from me. I felt a shirt being pulled onto me, and I nodded my hand in silent thanks.

When I glanced at Anthony and Mason, I saw two large bulges in their pants. I let a small smirk pass my lips, before sitting up lazily. As I did, I heard a small groan behind me.

When I turned around, I saw Luca and Dylan both with their pants and boxers down to their ankles. They each had a hand tightly wrapped around their large shafts, to which I gulped at the sight of.

It wasn't that I've never seen one before or I'm shocked, it's just that they were huge. I mean, huge, huge. When I took a closer look, they both hand their other hand wrapped as a fist around their head, and a small trail of something white came flowing from their fist.

I held back a laugh at it.

SEXUAL CONTENT ENDS HERE

All for boys glared playfully at me, which I returned with a small wink. But as I searched, I realized that Leo wasn't there. A small pang of disappointment rushed through me, but I brushed it aside. I stood up on surprisingly shaky legs, and flounced from the room, my sassy attitude was still on.

But as I passed Leo's room, I heard small grunts and moans coming from his closed door. Out of curiosity, I huddled closer to the door, to hear him calling out my name, followed by a sigh of relief. I smirked, knowing exactly what just went on. And in the back of my head, I knew everything was okay between us. We weren't damaged mates. We were close again. And I know he'll come to love my baby as much as i do. I sighed in relief at that, before continuing on.

As I closed my door, and went to the bathroom, I couldn't help but glance in the mirror, to no longer see a happy girl with her five best friends, but a young woman with a small baby bump and five, practically, husbands by her side. She looked loved.

I smiled, and for the first time, I felt completely, well, complete.

Respect

Mavis

A loud crash ricocheted throughout the house. I sprang from my bed, alert.

It's nighttime, 3 am to be specific. Everyone was asleep by this time. The crash sounded from the front door. The guys seemed to have heard the noise too, because I could hear four pairs of footsteps crashing down the stairs to the front door, where I could hear arguing going on.

Fear encased my body. What if one of my guys gets hurt? I opened my door to see Dylan ready to open it. I sighed in relief. At least one of my boys is okay.

As I thought this, another loud bang came from downstairs. Then gunshots sounded through the air.

I shrieked at the loud noises. Dylan tackled me to the floor and protected me instinctively. The ground under us shook from the noises and vibrations of the guns, and just as quickly as they started, they faded into the silent air.

I crashed down the stairs after my boys, the primal instinct to protect them kicking in. Adrenhaline shot through my veins, pumping through my system. I landed on the last step. I made my way down the halls. Mason trailed behind me.

I raced into the clearing of our entrance room. Standing there, Leo and Anthony were both covered in blood. I wasn't stupid. I knew it wasn't their own blood.

Which meant someone was in this house. Oh God.

Dylan and Luca were panting, and in between them, a body was limp on the ground. Blood leaked from nearly every part of the man's body. A gun rested next to him.

I shrieked in horror. I had to clamp a hand over my mouth to prevent the bile from coming out. How disturbing.

I ran to check on my boys. They were all luckily okay. "What the hell happened here?!" I shouted, ready to knock sense into them all.

Dylan moved swiftly towards me. He wrapped his slender arms around me, trapping me against his warmth. "Shhhh, it's okay. Everything is fine now," he murmured into my ear. He soothed me gently, cooing words to me. I trembled beneath his embrace.

I tried to shove Dylan away. He didn't let me go. He merely kissed me gently on the lips. He pulled me tighter to him, and nipped at my bottom lip, tempting me to open my mouth. I refused, hoping to punish him. He groaned in annoyance. Then I felt a second pair of hands grip my waist hungrily. I gasped in shock, allowing Dylan to shove his tongue in my parted lips, exploring all of my mouth.

The second body pressed tightly against mine, distracting me from every other thought. Dylan gently released his punishing hold on my lips. He smirked while backing away. I snapped out of my daze, as the second body also backed away. I was lucky my legs weren't jelly yet. I gasped, suddenly enraged at myself and those two boneheads for what they did. I slapped Mason harshly.

His face snapped to the side, shock was written on his face. He had a surprised look on his face, which quickly turned to anger. I felt a hand snatch my wrist, and jerk me away from the scorching glare of Mason, who now has a handprint that was bright red on his tanned cheek.

Leo jerked me to face him. I was surprised I didn't get whiplash from how harshly I turned. He was seething with anger. I didn't understand why. These men defiled me just because they think I'm weak and can't handle what's happening here. I can't believe them!

"Listen to me, you never slap your mates. Do you understand me? That dead man you saw, he was the man from the door a while back, the one that declared war. We found him on our doorstep this was with a few hunters. We're just lucky he's out of the way," he growled angrily. I still had shock on my face. This man was the alpha that declared war on us! I'm so relieved that we don't have that problem anymore. Although I can't believe what happened to him.

And did Leo just tell me what to do with my life? I snarled at him, pissed that he snapped at me. I poked my finger harshly at his chest. "Now you listen here! I'm your mate not some slut that you can just order around and then use for sexual fucking pleasure! That's not how this works. And if you think that then you can be my guest and leave! I want respect from my mates, and I can't believe that you would manipulate me like that. How is that respect? Until you can respect me, stay the fuck away. Got that?" I hate the fact that I practically told my mates to fuck off, in fact it broke my heart, but I will never take disrespect. Especially from people that I love so much.

The shock on their faces had me sighing in defeat. My heart tore. They really wanted me to just be obedient? Never. I huffed, before moving upstairs, and slamming my bedroom door closed. I quickly locked it.

I can't believe those incompetent men. Until they learn respect, I'm not coming out. They can blame themselves for me starving myself.

Maybe that's a bit much, muttered Uri.

I don't care, I snapped back. I didn't mean to be mean to her, I was just in a bad mood.

The loud knocking and pleading for me to unlock my door came all day and night, but I refused.

Not until they learn, I thought.

I'm Home

Mavis

"Please just let us try again! We never wanted to hurt or disrespect you! Please, baby!" Mason begged from outside the locked door, but I just turned up the volume on my speakers once again. I didn't want to hear anything he said. Not unless he got all the others up here to agree to give me respect, I wouldn't. What can I say? I have the pride of a bull.

The other guys gave up a few hours ago, but Mason never left the door. I have to say I'm really happy that he didn't leave. I don't know, it's nice to know someone cares for you enough to not leave. I have to say that I've had to bite myself, literally, to stop from opening the door. Bite myself. That's not natural.

Its only been a few hours, half a day at most. The sun still hasn't peaked over the horizon, and I blinked lazily out my window. I had only gotten an hour of sleep. Probably because Mason is awake too.

I sighed in defeat. I can't take this anymore. I got up, and stalked to the door silently. I threw it open, and Mason rushed in immediately. He wrapped his thick arms around my slim frame. He tightened his hold when I tried to pull away. I was still upset with him. I sighed in defeat once again, before wrapping my arms around him. My stomach had been staring to swell at the time, and I had almost forgotten about being pregnant. Haha, joking. You can't forget when you constantly feel like shit and you're throwing up buckets.

Mason pulled away gently, but kept me in his hold. I smiled at him cheekily. I knew it wasn't his fault. It wasn't any of my boys. But it was Leo. But what a hot, sexy creation. I had to admit, each of my guys had the impeccable ability to look like a supermodel that needs to return to their natural habitat, which was the magazines you see everyday.

I heard pounding footsteps, and I knew that Mason had contacted the guys. I hissed at Mason, fury clenching my heart painfully. How could he?! I can't believe him. I glared at him with pure anger, which he flinched away from. Guilt ate away at me, but I shook it away. He shouldn't've tried me.

I felt four other sets of arms wrap around me. Luca turned me to him, before smashing his lips on mine. I didn't have any time to react, before I felt a strong hand grip me tighter, and jerk me to them.

Anthony smiled lazily at me, before kissing me softly. His lips were warm and gentle. They weren't rough at all. He must really moisturize.

Dylan gently turned me to him once I parted from Anthony, and cupped my face lovingly. He smiled down at me. Love and affection shining in his eyes. He pressed his lips to mine. Dylan surprisingly had a rougher kiss than Anthony or Luca's. His lips were firm and harsh, but his entire being screamed difference. I kind of liked it.

Dylan gently let go, before turning me to my main compadre. Leo. His eyes had dark bags under them, and my heart strings felt as if they had been jerked around. I felt so sad seeing him like that. I couldn't bear it. I took the first step, and wrapped my arms around his shoulders gently. He seemed to stiffen at first, before he quickly pulled himself together, and wrapped his thick muscled limbs around my waist, and jerking me to him. His lips rested next to my ear.

"I will never do something so disrespectful again, mate. Never. I'm so sorry I ever said something like that. I've always respected your courage and bravery. I'll always love and respect you and our child and children." I froze.

He said it.

I cant believe it. Tears stung in my eyes.

He accepted my baby.

I screamed in happiness, before jumping on him, causing him to shout in surprise and happiness. We embraced each other gently. Our bond only seemed to grow stronger. My mates came around Leo, and stood next to me, each saying things that could no longer be described as just words.

We all made our way to the couch outside our front poor at the cabin, and we all watched the sun rise from the horizon happily. Us, as mates. As lovers. I knew I could never forget these moments. I would always fight for these men. And I would always love them. Sure, we would have some rough times. But never something that we couldn't solve together.

The sun kissed the sky happily, turning the cloud a beautiful blush. The horizon grew to a bright gold. Orange surrounded the gold, and the pink overtook all other color in the clouds. Beautiful. But I wasn't looking at that. I was looking at them.

My mates, I thought happily.

Im home.)

Epilogue

∧ I had to ^

I closed the thick book that rested in my hands. I glanced out at the sky.

I wish we had what these six did, I thought grimly.

"Thorne!" Zekar shouted from behind me. I turned my head to glance at him through the hoodie that rested on my head, covering my eyes. The tall, dark skinned man with cropped black hair smiled back at me.

"Did you finish that book?" He grinned cheekily. I sighed.

"Yeah," I called back.

"What was it called?"

I stood up from my resting position. I had to tell him about my book? And share about how there are certain scenes in here? That's hard. Although I skipped through them. It was too nasty for me. I've always been bad about things like that.

I glanced behind me. The once beautiful New York City was now in ruins. Fire was everywhere. Half the giant buildings were no longer standing in their full glory. Sirens echoed in the distance. Below, you could see small bodies running back and forth, some falling to the ground. The sky was dark. Night was coming.

I glanced back down at the book I held in my hands. Unfortunately, they never said what happened about Mavis and her mates. I was really pissed about that.

Zekar cleared his throat, raising his eyebrow. I sighed. "It was the legend of the Blood War. With the Blood Brothers and their mate."

"I knew it!" Shouted Zekar. I couldn't hold back the smile at my geeky mate. He always seemed to be so bright in these situations.

We stood seventeen stories above ground, in an old hotel. It was quite nice here with my mate Zekar. We were the only werewolves left, after all.

"I wish those six were still here. After the meteor strike everything went into chaos. The Blood Brothers had to hold back the vampires, since the vampires gained incredible powers with meteor strikes. Sadly, they all disappeared. I wonder what ever happened to them. It's been twenty years. Lord knows we could use their help," grumbled Zekar. I laughed lazily, before repositioning my knives so they were easier to access. "Well, sometimes shit happens." Zekar seemed to agree silently, the black armor he was wearing gleamed in the fires' radiant glow.

Gunshots were heard from below us. They're here. The vampires that destroyed all of humanity and all of the werewolves. I knew for a fact we were the only ones left they had to kill off.

Zekar gave me a knowing look. His smile was grim, but determined. With the number of footsteps underneath us, we both knew we wouldn't make it. But I think we were ready to die. There was nothing left in the world for us. No family from Zekar, mine disappeared. Now all I have left to remember them bye is this book in my hand.

I wiped away my fear-filled tears, and pulled out my throwing knives. Zekar shared a look with me. We both nodded.

One hundred footsteps away.

"Let's see what you can do, hm?" Zekar challenged me.

Ninety footsteps.

I took a deep breath.

Eighty.

I gave Zekar a playful glare, despite my nerves.

Seventy shots from death.

"I bet I can kill more," I jeered.

Sixty now.

Zekar huffed in amusement.

Fifty left.

He gave me a small smile, his eyes showing the true affection he had for me.

Forty mistakes made.

"I love you, Thorne," he murmured affectionately.

Thirty chances at falling in love.

"I love you too, Zekar."

Twenty at making it.

Zekar kissed me passionately, the taste of tears came from both of us. We were crying. We didn't want to leave each other. Not after everything we've been through.

Fifteen steps.

Zekar fixed himself, and gave me a supportive smile, despite his fear. I gave one back and positioned my knives.

Ten steps.

I brushed my tears away one last time.

And before those doors opened, I heard, "Let's see what you can really do, Thorne, daughter of the Blood Brothers."

The doors banged open, and my knives left my hands instantly.

The first two men fell. I kept up my pace, not stopping for a second. We were making amazing progress. Zeke shot them down with his mini machine gun, and me with my knives. I almost thought we could make it.

Almost.

I heard a cry of pain from beside me, and immediately whipped my head around to see Zekar. He was on his side, blood gushing from his chest. I let out a sob, my heart was breaking. My best friend, the love of my life. He was leaving me. No. No! NO!

I forgot about the enemies coming upstairs, and instantly threw a smoke grenade down the shaft. That should distract them.

I bent on my knees beside Zekar, and grabbed his face in my hands. I couldn't look down. It would hurt too much.

Zekar smiled at me shakily, before putting his hands over my own. They were pale. Blood poured from the bullet that lodged itself in his chest.

I couldn't hold back my sobs. The memories we had together, smiling, laughing, kissing, crying. They all came back. I didn't want him to leave. Not now.

I rested my forehead on his. "Don't leave me Zeke. Don't leave me," I begged quietly.

"I-I c-can't help it l-l-love." He cried out in pain once again. My heart couldn't take this. He pressed his lips to mine one more time. I could see the light leaving his eyes.

"I-I love you."

"I love you too Zeke!" I sobbed out.

He smiled happily, his eyes peacefully sliding shut, for the last time.

Red. That's all I saw. They were at the door now. I could feel the shot racking through my body, but I didn't care. I picked up one knife, and threw it at the first shooter. I kept this up for minutes, but it felt like hours. I knew I wouldn't last, but that didn't stop me.

I froze, as the next bullet hit me straight in the heart. I fell in my side, the last thing I saw was my beautiful Zekar. I held his hand tightly, pain racking through me. But I couldn't help my smile.

I can be with him.

I closed my eyes.

This is our reality. Two years after Mavis became pregnant from rape. That being me. After she gave birth to me, a meteor struck. Vampires took this chance to annihilate every single being in this planet, taking it for themselves. My family, which I was told it was the Blood Brothers and Mavis, disappeared after that. Zekar's family took me in, and I've considered them family ever since.

This is now. And I can't help but think, at least I'm safe now, before closing my eyes, and letting darkness overtake me.

Happy Epilogue

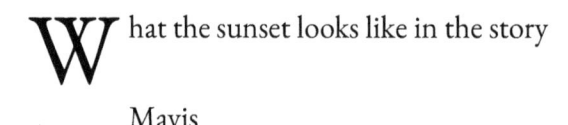

What the sunset looks like in the story

Mavis

I closed the thick book that rested in my hands, while unconsciously clicking my tongue.

A beautiful woman dressed in a pure white straight gown turned her sharp eyes to me. She smiled gently when she noticed the book in my hands. "I'm assuming you finished it?"

"Yeah, and I don't get it. I mean, what's the point of loving someone who doesn't even want you back?"

The soft looking woman with curly brown hair that was slightly greyed at the roots chuckled gently. "Don't say such insults to my first romantic book! I read that when I was 10!"

"MOM THERE ARE NASTY SCENES IN THIS!" I screeched, shock taking over my features.

"Don't be so loud," grumbled a deep, gravelly voice, as papa Leo stalked into the room. I sniggered silently at his grumpiness, before turning back to my mother. "Thank you, but I'd rather experience my own story with Zekar." Mom made an 'awwwww' sound and I blushed deeply.

"What are we awwing about now, hmm?" Papa Luca questioned as he walked by the opened kitchen door. "Girl stuff. Like periods and crap like that." I heard coughing come from the other room, and papa Dylan and papa Mason both peered into the doorway. "We'll leave it to ya then!" The room cleared quicker than I had hoped. My mother and I shared a giggle, before continuing our chat.

Half an hour after my encounter with my fathers, Zekar popped in to take me away from my family. I said goodbye, and we made our way to our small house on the edge of a cliff. I know, dangerous, but it's worth it when you see the sunrises and sunsets.

There was never a meteor strike, turns out the news station was faulty as fuck.

I lived happily by my mate, Zekar, and my parents. I know my fathers and I aren't blood related, but they treat me as their own and I love them. I have never been happier in my 23 years of life than I am now. By my mate's side.

Zekar carried me bridal style to the pure edge of the cliff, where the sun dipped to the horizon, lighting the atmosphere with warm hues of gold, orange, and pink. Thin clouds littered the sky above. The waves of the ocean below rippled across the jagged and rough rocks that hunkered at the bottom of the cliff. Zekar wrapped his thick arms around my small frame, and pulled me onto his lap. I blushed deeply as he wrapped his arms around my waist. He buried his nose into my hair, right next to his mark on my neck. I smiled as i placed my hands over his.

Zekar gently grabbed my chin, and turned my head to his. My body twisted with his pull. Once I faced him, he passionately clamped his lips onto mine. There was no need for a fight for dominance. He always won.

After kissing each other passionately, we both watch the fall of the sun, as darkness settles over the earth.

"Hey, Zekar?"

"Hmm?"

"Do you ever wonder what our futures will be like?"

He turned his head to watch me. His eyes were filled with love. "Sometimes, but I don't focus on it."

I tilted my head slightly. "Why not?"

He smiled. "Because, our story has just begun."